KRINGLE

KRINGLE

by

Derek Feuti

Visit our website **at www.StillwaterPress.com** for more information.

First Stillwater River Publications Edition
1 2 3 4 5 6 7 8 9 10
Written by Derek Feuti
Cover Photography © 2014 by Dennis Feuti
Cover design by Dawn M. Porter
Published by Stillwater River Publications, Glocester, RI, USA
ISBN-13: 978-0-69223-446-4
ISBN-10: 0-692-23446-2

Library of Congress Control Number: 2014943437

For my amazing parents, whose love and support made this possible.

And for Kim, because I promised.

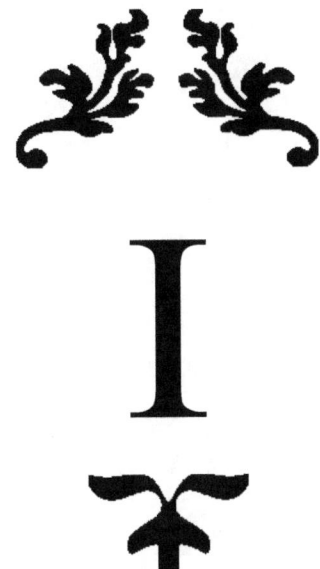

I

1

Estelle watched as the flurries came down, covering the forest floor in white. It was still spring, but winter's reach was long this close to the mountains. She rubbed her hands together as the fire beside her began to grow. The warmth spread slowly through her cabin, but it spread. Patience was a virtue she had learned to master long ago. If it were not for that, the dozens upon dozens of children – most orphaned as the fighting escalated – would have surely seen her collapse in upon herself under the weight of it all.

She had always wanted children, and when none came naturally she took in those who were suddenly without natural parents. The job fit her perfectly. Some still came around, but their visits were short and stitching up wounds lacked the enjoyment she found playing outside with them or teaching them their letters. Time changed all, whether elf or man. There was no discrimination. Estelle took some solace in that, at least. *Perhaps in enough time...* her thoughts drifted, losing their tangibility. It did not help to dwell on such things. *Not on a night like this.*

The forest was quiet as Estelle stepped out onto her front step. There were still the sporadic chirps and cheeps of the numerous insects that thrived even in the colder season, but even they seemed to take solace in the beauty of the night. She wrapped the cloth tighter about her shoulders but otherwise took pleasure in the crisp air. The trees around her home were young, not as tall and powerful as those she had seen as a child living deeper in the forest, but no less magnificent because of it. Behind them she felt safe, hidden from unwelcome eyes.

A cry brought her from the peace she had allowed to settle over her. It was not a deer or any other animal that called these woods home. Of that much she was certain. This was from the mouth of an infant. Estelle moved toward it as the cry turned to sobbing, using it to guide her through the maze of brush that grew thick around her. Others would have soon become lost in the veritable maze of upturned roots and low-hanging branches. But Estelle was an elf, and had lived in this land longer than many. And though she was not as fit and light on her feet as she had once been, she could still maneuver through the terrain with the grace endowed upon her race.

She stopped to steady her breath as the cries abated for a time. Fearing the worst, she continued in the direction she had heard them last and was rewarded as they started again close by. The snow was falling harder now. Estelle brushed off the flakes sticking to her clothes before they could seep in. Already she could feel the air growing colder. The ground opened up ahead as she neared one of the trade paths that once connected the many villages dotting the landscape. Most were now used to ferry weapons to the frontline, the wounded riding the wagons back. She stared down the empty road and listened. Nothing stood out as the babe continued its crying. *It should be here.* The sound was too close to remain out of sight. She yearned for the days when her eyes were able to pick out a chipmunk a hundred yards away. Now… *is not the time. Pining for the past won't help the present for either of us.*

Moonlight shone down as the clouds above drifted. She knew it would not last, so she took advantage of the gift. There was a knot of roots along the edge of the path belonging to an exceptionally large tree, given the size of the smaller roots beside it. *Then why do they thin out at the middle?* She made her way towards the anomaly, her pace increasing as the babe's cries grew nearer. The knots she had seen were not roots at all, but a cradle, woven with strands of wicker. Estelle bent low to get a better look and could not help but marvel at the workmanship put into its creation. The wood was of the finest quality and smoothed to perfection, a darker stain applied. The remnants of a ribbon still clung to the arch, flapping gently in the soft breeze.

The child reached his delicate hand out and she took it, feeling how cold it was. All else was forgotten as she gazed into his blue eyes. They appeared to shimmer in the light of the falling snow, unlike any she had ever seen in her long life. Tears moistened his round cheeks. She used the soft blanket covering most of the babe's body to wipe them away, singing an old lullaby her grandmother used to sing to her, when she noticed the stitching at the edge. A stag's head, the green thread standing out from the purple that made up the rest of the blanket. "What are you doing out here?" That and a dozen more questions ran through her mind. No answers presented themselves. There would be plenty of time for them later. "Let's get you out of the cold."

Estelle was able to take a quicker path now that she knew where she was going and arrived back in good time. A few inches of snow had already fallen. She tried her best to avoid the deeper parts at first but once her feet were wet it seemed unnecessary to keep at it. The babe was silent as she did her best to keep the basket steady against her thigh. The basket felt as if it weighed next to nothing, causing her to wonder at its maker.

The cabin had warmed considerably when she returned and for that she was grateful. The cold air had long since lost its appeal. Estelle placed the basket by the fireplace and removed the blanket, now chilled and damp. After checking to see if the cold had gone through to the child's clothes, she went to her spare room and returned with a drier set. "Now these may be a little big but at least they'll help keep you warm." The babe looked at her with those blue eyes, unwavering as she changed him – for it was in fact a boy – not once uttering another sob. His rounded ears came only as an afterthought. She was not of the mind that all humans were alike, each out to hurt those of the forest, but she was not the only one who would see him here. And the soldiers did not tend to share her feelings on the matter. *They wouldn't dare hurt a child.*

Or so she hoped. "I'll bet you're hungry." She returned him, wrapped tightly in the new woolen blanket, and walked to the kitchen.

Cupboards lined the wall above, each once filled to capacity with bowls and bottles, mugs and plates. Now they remained near-empty. Estelle did not need much to feed only herself. But she kept most of the bowls since they served more than one purpose. She sifted through the few glasses until she reached the narrow bottles at the back. She kept one even though there had not been a child so young in her cabin in years. What the future held was impossible to know. She found the rubber nipple beside it. Dust had accumulated on both, and she wiped them down before bringing them to the icebox.

Keeping things cold was never much of a challenge in these lands. The icebox was filled with crushed up ice and snow, the elf she traded with promising her nothing would ever melt once it was placed inside. As skeptical as she was, she knew that magick had once thrived in the world, with odds and ends still remaining from that time. True to his word, the ice remained as hard and cold as the day she filled it.

She took out a leather pouch and uncorked the stopper, pouring the milk into the bottle until it reached about the halfway point. She had planned to make tea with the water already boiling over the fire but decided she could wait. The bottle stood taller than the iron sides of the pot with most of the milk submerged. "Shouldn't be long, little one." The babe looked at her and for a moment she believed he actually understood her. But only for a moment.

A knock came at her door and her heart leapt to her throat. It was late and Estelle had not been expecting any visitors. She approached the door with caution though doubted there was much she could do should the visitors have ill-intentions. She opened the door and was relieved by the sight of hard leather beneath a red cloak. "Oh, Thysilar, I feared you were... it doesn't matter. What are you doing here so late?"

The elf stood a good foot and a half taller than Estelle, with his leather armor fitting close against his thin frame. He had his hood down, letting his long brown hair flow as it may. "I'm sorry to disturb you, Lady Kringle, but I wouldn't have come if it were not important."

Estelle only smiled, meeting his handsome face with warmth. He had been one of the orphans who stumbled into her care after his parents were killed when war first broke out. "You know you are always welcome. And that you don't have to use that name," she said.

Thysilar did not respond and it was clear to her that keeping pleasantries was not easy for him. Something was wrong.

"What is it?" Estelle asked. He parted to the side and allowed her to see the elves behind him. Two others, hoods up, were supporting a third between them. The cloth pressed firmly to his side was almost entirely bled through. "Bring him in," she said.

They needed no other word. Thysilar moved the sheet draped over the couch and helped as the others placed the wounded elf down. "You two keep watch. They may have followed." They obeyed his word without question. "What do you need?" he asked Estelle.

Her mind worked at its own speed, hardened from the hundreds of injuries she had witnessed. She was careful as she removed the cloth, revealing the laceration where a wide blade – likely a spearhead – had punctured through his armor. Her experience showed that, while better suited for their style of combat, the armor they wore was not ideal for fighting enemies such as the Falhofnans. "I'm not sure. If the blade took a piece of his undershirt along with it then there's a chance it's still inside. I'll have to remove it before stitching to avoid an infection." She spoke mainly to herself, but Thysilar nodded.

Estelle went back to the large shelf standing at the back wall of the spare room. She scanned over the dozens of bottles on the open square shelves before deciding on the two she needed. "Fill a bowl with some of the water by the icebox," Estelle said. She spoke loudly but the walls were thin enough and the rooms not particularly far apart so that Thysilar would have heard her even at a normal tone. A drawer underneath held the needle and thread she had used too many times. She kept a pile of hand cloths by the door and grabbed at them as she walked past, tossing one over to Thysilar. "Wipe away what you can." He dipped the cloth in the bowl and, after removing the elf's armor, started to clean the blood around the wound.

She rinsed her hands before getting to work. The wound was not as deep as she feared and did not appear to strike any major organs, but the spear had been wide and tore through a lot of muscle and flesh. He would not fight again for a few months, at least. The first small jar she uncapped had a powerful aroma that she had still not quite gotten used to.

"Hold him down." She was careful as she poured it into the wound. Such vials did not come cheaply.

The elf reacted as they all did, and Estelle was glad to have put the cork in his mouth to protect his tongue. Thysilar was able to keep his arms down but his legs were not as easy to control. He kicked out, striking Estelle in the hip and sending her crashing into the table at the middle of the floor. She steadied herself before the fall could become any worse. Thysilar looked ready to leap to her side when she waved him off. Bruises would heal. The elf calmed down, the worst of it over. The second bottle held a greenish paste of her own making that she applied once the wound was stitched. "He should try to rest as much as possible over the next week or so."

"I remember," Thysilar said. He sat in silence as she did her work and only now seemed to relax.

"So are you going to tell me what happened?"

"Ambush." Estelle stared at him until he realized she would not give up so easily. "There was a Falhofnan patrol. It was small enough we figured we could handle it."

Estelle was not convinced. "Just the four of you against a patrol?"

"There were nine of us." Thysilar stared at the fire as it died down. "We caught them unaware and were about to finish the job when two other patrols arrived. They must have been massing for an attack." He stood up and moved towards the basket. "Who's that?"

The babe had been quiet throughout the whole ordeal, and Estelle had nearly forgotten about him. Now that the panic was over and the elf mended, her mind was free to embrace this new worry. "Just another lost child."

"Where did you find him?"

The lie came to her quickly. "Left here like the others." She was glad now that she swapped out the blankets. "You know how these things are handled. The war has been hard on us all."

She was still busy cleaning up her supplies as the elf bent closer to the basket. A bottle slipped from her fingers and rolled around the countertop before she could pick it back up. There would be no hiding the child's truth.

Thysilar brushed a finger across the babe's cheek then froze. "He's human," he said softly, then repeated, slightly louder. The elf picked him up as he started to cry. "How could you allow *humans* to leave one of their own here? Have you forgotten what their kind's done to us?"

"Of course not," Estelle said, moving to take the child from Thysilar's arms. "Nor have I forgotten the things we have done to them. But this child is as guilty of those crimes as I am." *Another lie.* Only this one did not go down as well.

"I doubt the Falhofnans share your view."

"Either way he's my responsibility just like all the others who've passed through that door." Estelle took the bottle from the pot and waited before attaching the nipple. "Just like you were." There was nothing Thysilar could say or do to change her mind on this and they both knew it.

He stared daggers at the babe and pulled his hood up as it drank from the bottle. "I'll keep watch the rest of the night. Make sure the woods are clear."

She hated to leave things like this, but what could she say? Thysilar had his reasons to hate humans as did many others of their race. *He'll come around, in time. Once he sees the boy grow up, sees how different he is from the others. He'll have to.*

2

The crowds started to form. Gerold knew they would. The area at the base of the keep grew smaller as more and more of the people he now ruled steadily filed in. Chatter rose up to meet him in a din, each voice as indiscernible as the others. Rumors would spread like wildfire. The people were always eager for gossip regarding their betters. *Only they're my people, now.* That fact was not one he had stopped to give much thought to. Time had been in short supply over the last twenty-four hours. And his work was not yet finished.

The city of Falhofna had been built by the first men to settle the area, more and more of it added as the decades passed. Surrounded by an outer wall reaching forty feet, the city proper consisted of stone houses built to withstand the harsh, long winters those first settlers were forced to experience blindly. His eyes drifted towards the northern third of the city where such designs were yet to be implemented. As the population grew and construction was put aside to further the war effort, the area had become a slum. His predecessor tried to bring the workers back to finish the job but never managed to get much going. *Just another reason for change.* Between the main keep and the rest of the city was another wall, this one shorter. The keep itself was built from the very stone of the mountain it kept its back to. How his ancestors accomplished that feat was a mystery that none living could solve. The secret, it seemed, died long ago.

"And what of the rest of Niklas' personal guard?" Gerold asked. The former baron, for all he was lacking, had inspired a great deal of loyalty in the dozen men forming his inner circle. Each had proven themselves numerous times on the field. None had fallen alone. "We cannot afford a rebellion."

The young officer was not comfortable in his new position, and it showed. He could not have been past his sixteenth winter. Though such promotions were not uncommon for those his age, rarely did they go to men with so little experience. *If only the bastard had left a few more capable officers*, Gerold thought.

"Dead. Fled to the forests, Gen – my lord." Gerold could not blame him. The title of Baron was still new to his ears. The captain picked at his fingers.

"What is it?"

"The patrols we sent were hit by elves." The words were practically forced from his mouth. "There were casualties."

Gerold smiled. "Good. We can use that." Though the war had been going on for nearly a century, its popularity had not risen among the people. *That must change.*

The captain nodded nervously. "Very good, my lord."

"The elves were given enough chances for peace." The baron turned back to the window. An elderly man, his clothes dirty and disheveled, stumbled his way to the front of the group. His eyes peered up at the keep. "We have to protect our people." Gerold looked away from the man as his guards began to usher the mob back. "I want our patrols in that area doubled. These savages need to learn that there are consequences to murdering Falhofnan citizens.

"But my lord, our numbers are spread thin as it is. The garrisons cannot afford to –."

"You forget, Captain, that the elves killed beloved figures of Falhofna tonight," Gerold said. "Arrange a draft. The people lost their baron and will want to fight. Few things unify like a common enemy." The officer was dismissed and told to get what rest he could. It would be needed in the days to come.

Gerold let his fur cloak fall to the stone floor. The former baron's chamber was not much to look at. A large oak desk stood opposite him, lit by a pair of torches that were placed on either side. Loose papers and a few bundled scrolls dotted the floor, crinkling as he stepped over them. Gerold's men had caught the baron here. From the looks of things he was in the middle of writing his memoirs. Why the man needed so much ink escaped him. *Words can only accomplish so much. In the end it always comes down to steel.* He could not deny the power of words, but his eyes were set on larger game.

"That won't go over well with the king." Gerold slid the cushioned chair back and sat, not looking to the shadows where the voice came from. "Assuming the coup doesn't see you hung."

"The king will see things my way. He is not so foolish as to waste a man like me at the gallows." Gerold pushed the few pages still on the desk aside until finding the right one.

"Let's hope," the shadow responded.

Two soldiers entered the room unannounced. Gerold made out a glint of metal from the darkened corner. He shook his head, remaining subtle. The scouts were armored lightly, trading the protection of chainmail and plate for the speed and maneuverability of leather. Much of the design had been inspired by the elves' own armor. As cowardly as their tactics were, they had a talent for leatherwork that Gerold could not easily ignore. Both were young but not without skill. It was necessary for scouts if they hoped to last long in the forest. "My lord Baron," they said, "sir!"

"Calm down, catch your breath." Gerold placed the paper down atop the others and gave them a reassuring smile.

"Thank you, sir."

"Now what's so important that it could not wait until morning?"

"We were with the party sent out a few months ago, sir. To probe the base of the forest," the one on the left said. His face still bore the marks of youth, a trait his voice had moved past. "We were told to report immediately once we returned."

Gerold's mood turned serious. They should have returned weeks ago. "Where is your commanding officer? I remember giving that order to *him*."

"We're all that's left, my lord."

The words added to the weight on his back. He felt the papers crumple in his hands before a deep breath unclenched them. "Explain."

"We started where we were told, following the path deeper and looking for anything out of the ordinary, like you asked. All we found were animal tracks." Beads of sweat dripped down his forehead.

None of this was making sense. "I did not waste resources to have you lecture me on the local wildlife."

"It's just that we saw so many of them, my lord. It was impossible to see anything else. Even the elves left no sign." He wiped the moisture at his brow and continued. "We were ready to turn back when it started." The scouts' stares were empty. Gerold was quiet as he continued. "The trees… they took them. Everyone. Screaming and –."

The baron held a dagger in his hand before anyone else could react. He leapt across the desk with a speed that betrayed his armor and plunged the blade into the scout's throat. Brown eyes stared up at him, confused and scared. Blood dripped from his mouth as he tried to speak.

"No!" the second scout shouted, drawing his short sword.

Gerold was left open and defenseless, his blade still imbedded in the young man. He pulled the dagger free in a spray of crimson. The scout hit the floor as his partner closed in. Gerold turned to meet him, knowing that even if he reacted in time his shorter blade was ill-suited to go up against the scout's weapon. He watched as something blurred past and halted the scout's approach. The young man looked down at the hilt of a dagger protruding from his chest. His sword clattered against the stone as his grip slackened. Gerold watched, dagger held out before him, until the confused look on the scout's face faded. His body landed beside the other.

Anton stepped from the shadows, sliding a hand across his cleanly shaven head. He was a large man but moved no slower because of it. "We'll regret that. They were good scouts." He wore armor similar to that on the dead men, dyed black. The blade slid from the boy's chest with a single pull. He took out a kerchief and wiped the blood from the steel. "Here," he said, offering it to Gerold.

The baron did the same with his own blade as his anger began to subside. "Then others will have to rise and take their place."

"Of course, my lord." He refused the kerchief and pointed to Gerold's face. The scout's blood had gone unnoticed.

Gerold wiped it off as best as he could and crouched down, picking up the parchment he had knocked to the floor. "One good thing came out of this, however."

Anton returned the blade to its sheath at his side. "What would that be?"

Gerold spread out the map, keeping the edges pinned with jars of ink. He traced a path with his finger and stabbed his dagger into an area at the mountain's base. A drop of blood slid down the length, staining the paper. After years of arranging patrols, dozens of scouts lost... *I've found you.* His heart slowed back to its regular pace as his mind calmed. What he did was rash, but necessary. The stories had to remain stories. Magick was a myth, constructed by the savages as part of their barbaric religion. The king's own words.

Words that Gerold agreed with, of course.

3

The warm light of the morning sun bathed the area surrounding the cabin in an unusual heat. Vibrant greens and browns, oranges and reds caught the rays. The flowers never bloomed for long, though. The cold months never allowed it. But when the mountain calmed and its tendrils retreated back to its peaks, the forest's true beauty flourished. This was Kris' twenty-third summer and still he found himself drawn to the sight of them. He brought his axe down onto the block atop the stump, sending both pieces spinning end over end to the dirt. His hair was cut short, sweat coating his upper body. A thin layer of stubble lined his chin. He piled the new blocks with the others already stacked neatly against the wall of the cabin and placed another on the stump. The warm weather would not last forever. Kris twirled the axe handle over in his callused hands before bringing the blade down again.

"That should be enough for today, Kris. Come inside and wash before you get sick." Estelle stood just outside the door, looking old for the first time in all the years she had raised him. Her hair had thinned, with the natural brown strands now being outnumbered by

15

streaks of grey. She had never been particularly tall but Kris swore she had lost an inch or two. She always corrected him, saying if he didn't like it he should stop growing.

"Sick? Mother, there is hardly a cold breeze blowing." Kris smiled and picked up his shirt. He kicked aside the few remaining logs that he had yet to split, adding them to the unfinished pile.

"My Lady Kringle, may we..." The words caught Kris' attention and he turned away from his work. Two elves stepped out from the trees, their red cloaks draped over leather armor. Black-fletched arrows stood out from the quivers across their backs. He noticed links of chainmail where the pieces of leather separated. Those are new, he thought. They kept their hoods down and he recognized them as Thysilar's soldiers.

"You know my home is always open, Muriel," Estelle said, "What is it?"

Muriel stood shorter than most of her kind but Kris knew firsthand her skill with a blade was not hindered even slightly because of it. He still had a few bruises from their most recent bout. The other elf was less familiar to him, with a face he could not read. His arms were folded across his chest. "I wouldn't normally bring something like this to you, but I was hoping to find some more soldiers... I know how they tend to stop by here sometimes... and that you raised him..." Muriel's words trailed off along with her gaze. It was not like her to be so unsure.

Estelle did not push the question Kris could see burning within her. The same curiosity ate at him as well. *There were a lot of elves who grew up here*, Kris reminded himself.

Giving up on waiting for her to continue, the second elf spoke out himself. "Thysilar hasn't returned from his patrol."

Kris rushed over from the side of the house, revealing himself to the others. "What? Where was he? How long has it been?" Those thoughts and more flooded his mind, each vying for their own

16

attention. Estelle stepped over from the door and put her hand on his broad shoulder.

"Calm down," she said softly. "Let them speak."

If the elf thought anything of the intrusion, he did not show it.

"We had heard about a Falhofnan camp being set up not far from here. He thought they'd be a danger to you and decided it was best not to wait." Muriel had regained a measure of her confidence with each word. "We split into two groups, one to approach the camp and the other to wait until they tried to run before striking. They would have been caught on two sides."

"Not much of a fight, really," the other elf added.

Muriel ignored him. "We waited but, when none came, I ordered us in to see what was wrong."

"What did you find?" Kris asked.

Muriel looked over to him unbothered by the interruption. "Nothing. They were gone. The camp looked abandoned, as though everyone in it dropped what they were doing and just left."

Kris did not like how that sounded. If the camp was empty when Thysilar got there he would have called off the attack and regrouped. So why didn't he? "Could they have moved on? Maybe it was just a temporary camp for the night." He could taste the desperation.

"Not without us knowing," the second elf said.

"Halfar's right. The way things were left..." Muriel turned back to Estelle, darkness in her eyes.

Kris shrugged off the old elf's arm and walked inside the cabin.

"Where are you going?" Estelle asked.

"I have to find him." He was already in his room before her response could be heard. *He would come for me.* Though Thysilar was not kind with his views towards humans, Kris still looked up to him as an older brother. He would show up every few weeks or so with stories and news about things Kris had been too young to understand. Each time they caught him eavesdropping he was shoved out and told to play with his toys. He was thirteen the first time a chair was pulled out for him, their words kind instead of cold. The next day he was given a wooden sword and told his aches and bruises would go away if he practiced. He still remembered the look on Estelle's face when he tried on his first set of armor.

The leather he strapped on now was bigger than most, specially made to fit someone of his size. At over six feet he stood taller than every other elf he knew. He looped the small quiver over his shoulder along with the bow Khalen had given to him his sixteenth winter. The short sword was last, Kris testing its weight before belting it around his waist. He took up his brown cloak and left. The red was a mark only granted to the elves. He had asked Estelle about it one night but was warned never to bring it up again. She yelled at him before when he was young and misbehaved as all children do, but this had been the first time he had seen her truly upset.

Estelle and Muriel remained where he had left them. Halfar stood at the tree-line, his hood up. He stopped by the woman who had been his mother, his blue eyes fixed on hers. "If the others haven't found him, how can you expect to?" she asked. There was no harshness to her tone. Only honesty.

"I don't know," Kris said. And he didn't. "But I have to try. You know he would if it was me."

Estelle was quiet as she hugged him, her short arms barely able to reach all the way around. "Just be careful."

Kris smiled, squeezing just a little bit harder. "I love you too."

"The boy's coming with us?" Halfar asked as they walked past him.

"I'm not a boy," Kris said.

The elf smiled, amused. "So young. All of you. By the time you even begin to grasp the world around you, you are buried in it."

"There'll be time to discuss philosophy later. We should move while there is still sunlight." Muriel pulled her hood up over her head and took point.

Kris had ventured into the woods before, both while being taught to hunt and then on his own whenever Estelle would let him go. The bow was not his strongest talent. Never before had he gone this far. The sounds he heard at night while trying to sleep were all around him now and seemed all the more real. When he was younger his imagination would run wild with great monsters behind the dozens of cheeps and howls. Even now, many years older, he found his head filled with those images once more.

Muriel and Halfar kept a difficult pace to match. Kris knew that the elves could maneuver this landscape better than any but witnessing it with his own eyes was entirely different. Every part of their bodies moved with a graceful purpose, appearing to glide over the leaf-strewn ground with ease. Nothing was disturbed. Each broken twig and dry leaf made Kris feel all the more foolish for thinking he could be out here with them. They had decades of training and a natural ability that he simply did not. It was not an easy fact to accept. Though neither of them said so, he felt sure he was slowing them down. They rarely stopped to rest and he would not dare speak out about any discomfort.

After what felt like hours, they arrived at the abandoned camp. The Falhofnans had made camp in a small clearing not far from the mountain's base. It was a wise tactic, guaranteeing one less area that any attack might come from. *Except in this case.* Kris had never seen the aftermath of a real battle before but strongly believed something like that had taken place here. Bowls and spoons lay unceremoniously scattered in the dirt, left where they fell. A pot of burnt stew still hung over the blackened remains where a fire once burned. All that was missing were the bodies. He stepped over an upturned stool to join the others at the center. "So where should we start?"

The elves were silent for a moment as Halfar crouched down to look at something in the ground that Kris could not see. He picked at the loose material at the hilt of his short sword with his thumb, waiting. There was no other noise. In all his life here he had not once known a moment so quiet. The forest was normally so alive. Estelle used to say that it was smarter than even elves believed. *So what's it trying to tell us?*

"Come here and have a look," Muriel said.

Kris bent down to try and see what they were showing him but only saw dirt. There were a few marks but nothing that resembled any tracks he had ever seen. Halfar exhaled through his nose and stood. "The boy doesn't even know what he's looking at."

"I told you before that I'm not a boy." Kris said, feeling defensive. What did they expect of him? He said that he would help find Thysilar, not name every little imperfection that they came across.

"Then prove me wrong. What does that look like to you? A boot? Because if so you'll need to show me who it is with feet so narrow." Halfar was frustrated, Kris could see that much. He had been friends with the elves that were now missing and the mystery of it all was taking its toll.

He knew that but still he stood, letting his anger influence him. "There's one boot I wouldn't mind showing you."

Halfar's amused smile returned. "Try it, boy. Nothing would give me more pleasure right now than to teach you the respect Thysilar clearly didn't."

At the mention of Thysilar Kris felt his hand dart to his sword, unable to stop it. What would have happened if Muriel did not step in he chose not to think about.

"Enough! This is solving nothing." She exchanged a few soft spoken words with Halfar and watched him until his stance loosened and he elected to see if the same disturbance was anywhere else. "Don't mind him. All of this is just –."

"It's fine, I get it." Kris said, wishing he had better control of himself. *I'm not the only one looking for a friend*, he thought. "So what is it I should be looking at?"

Muriel brought him back down and pointed at the deep gash in the dirt. "This. It's from a root, dug out of the ground."

He was unsure how that was supposed to make any more sense to him. "The Falhofnans could've dug it out to make space for their camp. It's right in the middle."

"No." Muriel said without hesitation. "This one wasn't visible and wouldn't have even been able to trip anyone."

"So it just decided to dig itself up and move?" Kris asked with a short laugh.

Muriel only looked at him. She stood back up and began to follow a line that apparently only she could see. There was another disturbance a few yards away, this one much smaller and not the same shape. The track brought them both deeper into the woods again until they came upon a large patch of ground that was completely torn up. "Here." she said as though the entire mystery was solved.

Kris stared in silence until he could no longer take it. "'Here' what? What's here? It's just a hole." Large though it was, with layers of disturbed earth standing out darker than the rest around it, it was still just a hole.

"A hole where a tree used to be."

That gave him pause. "So...I was right?" Estelle told him stories at night, many of which dealing in some degree or another with magick and how much more present it used to be in the millennia past. After each he would ask where it went but Estelle never had an answer. *'And then the trees uprooted, bringing their shade along with them.'* How the rest of the story went he could no longer remember.

"I never admitted you were wrong." Muriel said as she walked around the length of the hole. "Though I'm not sure this really answers any questions. Even if the trees really did act on their own to get rid of the Falhofnans, why would they do the same to Thysilar and the other elves? We're fighting to defend the forest."

"I didn't think magick like this still existed."

"It isn't supposed to. Our people would have known. We would have felt it."

Kris did not know what to make of any of this. He always wished those stories were real but never actually believed it could happen.

"We need to see how far they go." Muriel said. "Keep following this one and double back once you don't see anything more."

"By myself? What are you going to do?" he tried his best to sound confident.

"To tell Halfar what we found and send him to check the east. I'll go south." She waited a moment longer and gave him a reassuring smile. "You'll be okay. Just remember everything Thysilar and the others taught you." She started walking away before turning around. "And try not to get turned around. The trees can play tricks on the weary."

Kris chuckled to himself and looked down at the hole. He found something that looked like it could be the same sort of track that Muriel had been following and started walking. *Right. Don't get lost. Easy enough.*

4

Eyes followed them down every road. Hungry stares glared at the polished armor like it was a banquet. *They know how much food even one of these suits would buy,* the baron thought. The half dozen knights at his back wore their fur cloaks over the plate, each skinned from one of the large bears that lived in these parts of the north. Gerold opted out of his armor, instead wearing the black pelt over a fine cloth doublet. The symbol of his barony – the head of a grizzly bear – was stitched into the left breast. A thin crown of silver and inlaid sapphires rested on his head. He scratched at his beard which had more grey than he cared to admit. *Over twenty years and still they look at me like a stranger.*

The renewed war effort had meant increased taxes, and despite his numerous attempts at humanitarianism, that was something the people had not gotten over. *I keep them safe, finish building their school, and House of Physicians. Still they can only think of their own coin.* One of his knights was approached by a haggard old woman clawing at his cloak. She begged for some copper, bread, claiming she had children starving and sick. It was an old song that

Gerold had grown tired of hearing. He watched as the knight shoved her aside with the butt of his spear. No one was there to catch her.

Gerold pulled up on the reins of his horse as a line of children crossed in front of him. They cast wearied glances his way but did not linger long before returning their eyes to the back of the person in front of them. Their teacher kept them moving, flashing a smile the baron's way. "Stay in line. Jacob, Erik, you know what I told you before." Two boys towards the back of the line stopped their horseplay and bowed their heads. The baron smiled as he saw them continue to jab and kick at each other when the teacher was not looking.

They continued on through the market. The square was busy despite the economic troubles, Gerold continued to be pestered about. It was not like he could make the crops grow or create gold from iron. He nodded and waved at his people, occasionally receiving the same in return. A guard column marched past on their way to the armory. The outer wall was stationed with a man every twelve feet, every six for the inner surrounding the main keep. The promise of steady coin and food had brought more recruits while the draft brought the rest. There had been the beginnings of riots and whispers of revolt, but the idea of facing down armored knights on horseback turned them away. If a few had to die to keep the peace.... The cost was cheap in comparison.

Gerold left his horse with the stable boy and returned to his chambers. His desk was home to a constant pile of papers and letters from his staff and council, each asking for one thing or another. There was a never ending stream of demands and only his one mind to handle them all. *It's no wonder Niklas hardly left his study.* He rested his cloak at the back of his chair and sat down, feeling the headache that was sure to come. Captain Dmitri entered shortly after, his interruption a welcome one. "I'm aware of the situation in my own city." Gerold stated curtly.

In the years since his promotion he had grown into both his position as well as himself. He stood tall and thin, with long arms that made him all the more deadly with the longsword belted at his hip. His face still retained the youthfulness he had come to be known for among the other officers. "I only say them to remind you of the second half of your duty. The people must not be forgotten."

"And they haven't been. It's their strength and sacrifice that has gotten us this far."

"It's that same sacrifice that could see your rule challenged." Dmitri said.

Gerold set his quill down over the ink pot. "Is that a threat, captain?"

"What? Of course not, my lord! I only point out a potential danger. You've seen what happens when the mob grows tired with their ruler."

He only meant to speak openly, Gerold knew, and his advice was one the baron had tried to remember to heed. His eyes drifted over to Anton who sat by the fire, running a whetstone over one of his knives. Age had not robbed him of his mass nor proficiency. The captain was no threat. "Look out that window," Gerold said. "What do you see? People angry with their lives here? Those willing to take up whatever arms they can in rebellion? No. What you are looking at is control. Order. What you are looking at… is peace."

"Yes." Dmitri said. Anton slid the stone along the blade, piercing the silence. "Forgive me."

"You know that I'm always open to advice from my officers, captain. Never hesitate to speak your mind in these walls." Gerold picked up the quill and went back to writing yet another response for a local steadholder. "How else will I be able to correct you?"

"Of course, my lord. Thank you."

"You're dismissed."

Anton waited for the captain to leave before speaking. "He's right, you know. Oppression rarely ends well for the oppressor."

"What do you know of it?" the baron asked. He was reading through another of the king's direct letters – the fifth to be sent in the past year. They all said the same thing and Gerold was running out of reasons to put them off. The king was not happy with the way the war was going. The other barons and nobles agreed, if the words were true. *What can't they understand? It is going to take time to bring the savages to their knees. I only inherited this war.* The loss of life was regrettable but also unavoidable. He was working towards something far more valuable.

"History is a fine enough teacher." Anton said.

"And what do you think history will teach of me?" Gerold asked.

Anton smiled, not foolish enough to fall into a similar trap as Dmitri. The tip of the knife slipped, drawing a bead of blood from his thumb. "That, my lord, is entirely up to you."

Gerold moved the parchment aside. He pinched the bridge of his nose in an attempt to stem the flow of thoughts and issues all vying for his focus. When he opened his eyes Anton was looking at him. "And of you?"

"I'm not much for books." he said in his unshakably calm tone. "History has no place for those like me."

Neither of them spoke as the baron continued sifting through his papers. He ignored most of what he could, piling them where he would remember to reply later. The jug of wine at his desk was nearly empty. He poured what was left into his goblet and took a generous sip. "The latest party of scouts have returned."

Anton focused on another of his blades. "And?"

"Nothing." Gerold said. "And I'm running out of time."

Anton turned at the whispered words. "Sir?"

27

The baron finished what was left in his cup and leaned back into his chair. The number of 'X's' on the map in front of him had grown heavy following the mountain. "Every group we've sent have returned broken, if at all. It's up there. It has to be. And something is keeping it from me." He swept the papers on his desk aside in a sudden outburst. He reached for his cup and tossed it against the wall as he remembered it was empty. "I cannot fail here, Anton. If the king's armies are unable to deal with these savages, what's to stop our enemies in the east from invading? There'll be blood in the water. And the sharks will keep coming."

Anton stood and sheathed his knife. "Let me go."

"What?" Gerold asked, unfocused. The palms of his hands were rubbing against his eyes. He could not recall the last time he had truly slept.

"I'll take a small team of my best. I've sat behind these walls for too long."

The baron wanted to dissuade him. His skill was without question and for that reason he could not afford losing him. But he was right. Before attaining his title, Gerold had used the scout for every high priority assignment. The risks were there, but the results were unquestionable. *The unused sword grows dull.* "Go."

Anton left with only a nod.

Gerold stood in front of the fire after his scout left and stared at the flag hanging above it. His insignia stared back down at him, fierce as it had always been. He held out the papers in his hands and looked down at the royal seal at the bottom corner of each. *You can't keep it from me.* The fires spread along the dried ink, surrounding the wax before it too succumbed. *Not anymore.*

5

Everything looked alike. Kris followed the trail of broken earth for what felt like hours and started to doubt the validity of what he was looking at. Moss hung from the branches above creating a curtain that limited his vision to just over a dozen feet. *Great.* He was growing impatient. All the great stories he heard the elves tell, filled with daring and excitement, victories through battle. None of them ever mentioned the frustration that the forest could cause. *Not exactly the stuff of tales.* He used his sword to hack at a bundle of low-hanging branches and continued.

The ground was broken up by scores of roots, large and small, threatening to drag him down if he was not mindful. The trail was near-impossible to find. Kris was ready to turn back and see how the others had fared when a cry cut through the chatter of wildlife. It was faint at first, only enough for Kris to stop. He listened, gathering all of his focus for another sign of the sound. He felt his heart race at what the possibilities of the shout might mean. Assuming he had even heard anything in the first place. Minutes passed by in complete stillness. The birds above sang their song.

And the shout came again. Clearer now, Kris distinctly heard the word 'help.'

He turned in the direction he guessed it was coming from and ran. The roots beneath posed little threat as he moved, his pace determined. A cold wind rose the closer he came to the mountain, and there was little doubt that was where the voice was leading him. Thysilar was there. No other thought entered his mind. The third shout confirmed it. The voice could belong to no one else. He pushed his way through a patch of brush, ignoring the small cuts and scrapes from the sharper thorns. A thin elven frame was leaning against a pile of rocks that had gathered at the base of an incline. Dirt and bits of blood stained his clothes and exposed skin. Something had torn through his armor, revealing the pale flesh beneath. Kris almost did not recognize him.

"Thysilar!" He rushed over to his friend's side.

Thysilar had never been a large figure, but to Kris he looked even more fragile. He had only been missing for a little over a day though he appeared as dehydrated and malnourished as if it were weeks. The act of turning his head took more than he had left to give. He tried to speak but only a dry whisper reached Kris' ears. "No."

"I heard you call out. The others are looking for you, too. You and the elves that were with you." Kris was filled with more excitement than he had felt in years. Thysilar was in bad shape but he was alive. Kris had a measure of faith but the facts were still piled against it. He felt the weight of it in his chest growing the further into the forest he went. But now it was gone. His friend was alive. "Can you move?" He knew the answer before finishing the question. "That's fine. I can carry you to the camp. I think I remember the way." Kris took a glance around. *Right. I don't even know how I got here.*

Thysilar's eyes never left Kris. They stared, open, almost pleading for the words his mouth could not form.

"What is it?"

And then he heard. Not the whisper or the imitated cries that brought him here – Thysilar could barely speak, let alone shout. No. The sound he heard now was growling. His fingers gripped the hilt of his short sword as he dared to turn. The wolves of the wood were not beasts to be dealt with without caution. He felt the weight return to his chest, pound by pound. The pack was five strong, from those he could see. The largest of them stood at the forefront. Most of their breed came up just past his knees, slim but with enough muscle to take down a full grown horse on its own. The Alpha was different. It stood at least three times the size of the rest of its pack, its coat parted with the scars of numerous wounds. Leadership had not come easily. Blood-red eyes stared down wide snouts. They had set a trap. *And I walked right into it.* Thysilar's only word made all the more sense.

Kris shrugged the bow from his shoulder and let it land on the ground. It would only hinder him here. The wolves spread out in a half circle, not once taking their gaze off of him. Backed against the mountain there was not much he could do. He was on their terms.

His sword slid free in one deft motion, the tip pointing at the Alpha. The elves had gone hard on him, true, but Kris knew none of them had ever given him their full strength. Even Thysilar, who never pulled any punches knew when and how to restrain himself. Now here they were. Deer were one thing. From a distance, with his bow, he could take his time, wait for the perfect moment. This would be much different. This enemy would be trying to kill him. Kill them. "Come on then!"

The Alpha snarled as the others charged.

Kris hit the ground with force enough to knock the air from his lungs. The wolf on top of him snapped at his face and throat. He smelled the old blood and meat on its breath. Warm spittle struck his skin. He managed to keep the brunt of its attacks at bay with his forearm but could do nothing as its nails raked against his body. The boiled leather held but more than a couple made it through. He tried to remember what Thysilar and the others had told him when they sparred. Something had to apply here. But as its claws found the weakened sections in his armor's seams, easily cutting through the cloth and flesh beneath, his mind refused to focus. The pain, fresh and unfelt before now, took hold. He knew he should push through it. Take that pain and use it to guide him through the fight and leave him standing, the victor. He knew all that and could only think of the life he was leaving behind.

Estelle, with her clothes and hands covered with soil as she worked in her gardens.

The smell of the meals she would cook, of new spices and seasonings bought from her annual trips to the larger elven towns.

She promised he would get to accompany her when he got older. And then he saw Thysilar. The elf was broken, far from the proud warrior Kris knew him to be. All the fierceness and passion was taken from him. He had been beaten. What chance did Kris have where Thysilar and the other elves had failed?

Kris pushed with some of the little strength he still had and avoided another bite. He could not keep it up. The next one may not find its mark, but he was not so confident about the one that would follow it. His right arm still gripped his sword. Trapped under the weight of the wolf it did little good. *Why aren't the other wolves tearing me apart?* The thought puzzled him until he realized it did not matter. They would sooner or later and he would be just as dead. The wolf bared its teeth in aggravation and reared back, preparing for another lunge. He refused to close his eyes. He had gotten himself into this mess and would not shy away from the consequences, whatever they happened to be. The wolf's head came down faster than he was ready for and overpowered him. Despite his confidence he flinched.

The wolf cried, its teeth never finding him. Kris shook off the moment of shock. He had to act. With a loud shout he pushed the beast away and freed his other arm. The blade slid across the wolf's stomach. There was another cry, this one longer and more pained. Warm blood fell onto Kris' arm with drops splashing onto his face. He could not falter. He kept up the momentum and pinned the wolf to the ground. Its eye glared up at him as he drove his blade down. The cries stopped.

Kris stood from his knees with his blade out before him. The rest of the pack only stared. *This prey will not fall so easily.* He was not the only one to share that thought. He turned as Thysilar dug through the rocks by his side for another that could fit in his hand. There was another similar to it by his feet. The elf must have struck the now dead wolf before it opened his throat. Neither of them would go down alone. He doubted Thysilar would be able to do more than slow any of the others, assuming he even hit his mark again, but it was comforting to know he had an ally.

The Alpha uttered a series of quick growls as though giving orders to his remaining pack. The other wolves howled once in response. They had learned. Kris would not be so lucky as to face them one at a time. They charged as one with the Alpha in the lead. "Come on," he whispered over and over to himself. "Come on and be done with it."

He raised his sword, ready to swing, when the wolves were stopped in their tracks. The branches hanging above had dropped down like so many snakes, lashing and wrapping themselves around the beasts. Kris stood still in silence and could only watch as the roots of nearby trees ripped through the hard earth to join the fray. One wolf was dragged off into the forest, its howls growing softer until they could no longer be heard. Another was beset on all sides and pulled up into the brush above. The Alpha took a slap from a root but moved along with the blow. It swatted another aside with its paw before biting down at a branch that tried to wrap around its neck. The limb split under the pressure. Two more were turned to kindling before the mass of roots and branches lunged out together. The wolf could not stop them all. It was quiet as they carried it off, red eyes burning bright in the shadows.

Kris was still standing where he'd been when the trees shifted their attention. The confidence he felt after killing the first wolf had dissolved. How was he expected to defeat the might of the forest? Branches reached out for him only to meet the sharp end of his blade. One, two, twelve, none of it mattered. Their numbers were many and inexhaustible. The best he could hope was to keep them away from Thysilar. He sliced through a cluster of roots at his feet and ran. All around were enemies. Cuts opened where his skin was less protected. He slashed through those he had to but otherwise relied on his speed. *I just have to draw them far enough away. They'll forget about him. They have to.* Kris did not know how far he made it before the roots at last tripped him. He hit the ground and swatted desperately as the living host grabbed at him. He felt pressure around his wrists and ankles before being taken by the all-consuming and impenetrable darkness.

6

The warmth of the sun caused Estelle to regret wearing long sleeves. She dug her fingers into the loose soil and pinched at the root of a weed. It offered little resistance. She tossed the plant over with the others, already looking for the next. Her garden spread out along the edge of the clearing at the side of her cabin. Sunlight did not breach through the canopy of leaves above in enough potency anywhere else and even here she had had to climb and trim some of the branches herself. Kris had offered to do it for her those years ago but she did not allow it. *I should have known then the type of man he would grow up to be.* He was so like many of the other boys she had raised. *Adventure is in their blood.*

She watched a spider move across the dirt between plants. A ladybug landed on the petal of a rosebush. All citizens of her little kingdom. And she was their queen. *No. This land already had a queen. Look at all the good she did.* Estelle took up her shovel and dug out the plants that she saw would not live out the coming winter. She would pick up more seeds during her next trip into Brindarry. Her harvest had been bountiful this season and her crops were popular amongst the other traders. There may even be enough to replace some of her gardening tools. Her shears had grown dull and rusty.

The rest of the afternoon passed and Estelle continued her work. Her mind had to stay busy. *They should have returned by now.* She packed up her things and brought the box back to the shed she had made during her first few years here. The lock on the door refused to click. She was growing more and more frustrated when she slammed it into the wood, reaching her boiling point.

"I don't seem to remember that working very often."

Estelle turned at the voice. Her anger remained. "What are you doing here?"

The old gnome was short, his bald head reaching her waist. He smiled through his snow-white beard and laughed. "Is that any way to greet an old friend? It's been nearly two centuries. I expected at least a hug."

Estelle forced the lock closed and turned back toward the front of the cabin. *Two centuries wasn't nearly enough time.* "I suppose we remember things differently."

"You can't still be upset about that. You know the reasons as well as I. It was what had to be done." Feltahn's voice brought back memories even without the words it spoke.

"If you don't mind, I'd rather you say whatever it is you feel must be said and leave. This day has been long enough."

The gnome's smile never faltered. "It's always hard when they take those first steps into the world. I remember watching my son do the same." His eyes drifted, but only for a moment. "They all yearn to have stories told of them until the wild becomes real. The best we can do is hope they'll find a guide."

Estelle stopped a few feet behind him. "How did you know about Kris?" She knew the answer without having to hear it. *Of course.* "What have you done with him?"

"Nothing he hadn't already done to himself, I promise."

"I'm in no mood to hear about Fate."

"That's fitting; I have no desire to speak of it." Feltahn said. "There's always a choice."

His words sounded the same now as they had then. *And they're just as hard to believe.* "If you've hurt him –."

Feltahn continued as though not hearing her. "You stopped wearing it."

"What?" she asked even as her hand reached for the bare patch at the base of her neck. "It was too heavy."

He changed the subject back as quickly as before. "I only came here to tell you your boy is safe. I know how much he means to you."

Estelle felt a weight leave her chest, if only for a moment before the rest of his words sank in. "So he'll be staying with you, then," she whispered to herself. There was nothing else she could do to have him brought back to her. If there was one thing she could always count on with Feltahn it was when he did something, he did so with complete surety in his actions. There was no looking back. She fought back a shiver as a cold breeze blew from his direction. She wiped back the tear from her eye, hoping he hadn't noticed.

He crouched and brushed his hand against one of the roses. For the first time his smile paled. "You always wanted children."

Estelle turned towards him but he was gone. She went over to the rose he touched and wiped away the frost that had formed. The light of the dwindling sun was fading. A rustling in the woods caused her head to whip around and for a moment she thought everything the gnome had said was just a lie. Muriel and Halfar entered her clearing with a third figure held between them. Estelle knew without a doubt it was Thysilar. She felt a portion of the weight in her chest disappear and scanned both beside and behind them for Kris. The closer the three elves came, the more of her hope left.

"My lady, where can we put him?" Muriel asked. Exhaustion lined her face and laced her voice.

"Put him on the couch." Estelle said. She led them to the door, quieting her mind with each step. There was nothing that worry could accomplish. Kris' life was no longer in her hands. The day would come, she knew. It always did. Her focus had to be on Thysilar, a child she *could* help. She opened the door for them when the injured elf stopped, reached out, and grazed Estelle's shoulder. His words were too faint to hear. "Don't try. They'll be time enough later." She stepped aside and let them in. Darkness had descended on the woods. The beasts of the night would wake soon.

Thysilar's wounds were many but aside from a gash along his side none were overly serious. Estelle washed her hands with a wet cloth and brought the bowl and other things she had used outside. The other elves were waiting. Halfar looked up from the arrow he was toying with and patted Muriel to get her attention. Estelle told them everything was fine and that all Thysilar needed now was rest. They thanked her and left. The others would want to know what happened. So would I. But her curiosity would have to wait. She sat in her chair by the couch and caught herself dozing off more than once. In spite of the events of the last day, she was exhausted. The hours went on and she no longer tried to stop it.

She woke in the middle of the night to the sounds of coughing and felt dizzy as she stood too fast. Her arm rested on the arm of the chair as she allowed her body to catch up. Thysilar looked around in a temporary panic before realizing where he was. He looked at Estelle and exhaled, resting his head back down on the pillow. She scooped some ice from her cold-box into a cup and poured water up to the lid. Thysilar was grateful for the drink. Estelle let him finish before talking.

"What can you remember?"

He was slow to respond and when he did his voice was heavy. "We heard the Falhofnans screaming. The attack wasn't supposed to start yet, so I led my group in thinking the others had come under attack. It wasn't us." He bit down on a piece of ice. "Wolves had descended on the camp. A pack larger than any I had seen. And…the trees. It was difficult to believe what we were seeing. I – we shouldn't have lingered as long as we did."

"They turned on you as well." Estelle surmised. The wolves of the forest were not scared easily and if the pack was large enough, Thysilar and his elves would have looked like nothing more than a meal.

Thysilar nodded. "We killed off more than half of them but not without cost. The Falhofnans were not all dead and took the distraction as a chance to act. By the end only two others still stood beside me. The wolves wore us down, one by one, until I collapsed. They were circling me before Kris came." He shifted uneasily out of discomfort before settling down again. "He killed one but I was not foolish enough to believe he could handle the rest." Even as he spoke she could see that he struggled to take what he saw as the truth. "The forest came to life. The roots, branches, all of it. The forest saved him."

Estelle felt a cool breeze blow in through the window over the couch. Gooseflesh spread across her skin. *No, it didn't.*

7

Kris was unsure how long he had been out. Consciousness returned to him, bringing the pain his adrenaline had pushed away. His eyes stung, unable to focus, and he kept them closed for a while longer. He was lying on the ground. That much he could tell. A blanket kept him from the dirt. The lack of pressure on his body told him his armor had been removed. He lifted his arm, fighting through the aches it caused. The clothes he wore were not his own. Reaching up under his shirt he could feel the cuts suffered from the wolf's claws. They had been treated, the area layered with an almost wax-like cream that had hardened. It made moving difficult. He was taken in by someone and, for whatever reason, had been given care. Whoever that person was had answers to more than a few questions and he intended to learn them.

The soreness in his eyes still lingered but he could wait no longer. It was not as bad as it had been. He was in a small tent, his gear piled neatly by his feet. A stool stood behind his head with a jug of water atop it. The sight caused him to realize how dry his throat was and without thinking he lunged for it. He felt the sealant on his wounds resist the sudden movement and pinch at his skin. His muscles also took this moment to voice their disagreement. He fought down a shout and stopped, taking deep breaths.

"Why the rush? The water isn't going anywhere." The gnome stood at the doorframe and stroked at his beard. Kris was startled by the voice and unexpected appearance of his host. "It's not considered polite to stare, you know. I thought Estelle would have taught you that."

At the mention of his mother he found himself defensive, the kindness already shown him forgotten. "What do you know of her?"

"More than most," the gnome said. "The wolves were not meant to find you. Sometimes their appetites are a little larger than I'd prefer."

"*You* sent them? They nearly killed me." Kris would have shouted if his voice had not been so hoarse. He took his time in picking up the jug and took long gulps, nearly choking more than once.

"They were the only thing that kept your friends safe. The Falhofnans were in greater numbers than the elves thought. And more than that, they were ready for them." The gnome pulled aside the tent flap, letting the sun shine in. "These elves… they think they can ambush an enemy in the same way a hundred times over and that same enemy will not catch on. Everything else that's said about you humans, you know a thing or two about waging war."

Kris raised his hand to shield his eyes. A dozen questions needed to be asked but he only gave voice to one. "Who are you?"

The gnome smiled as though pleased with the question. "My name is Feltahn. I would've brought you to my home straight away but as you'll learn, the wildlife is… sparse, the further up the mountain you climb."

"No one can live on the mountain," Kris said.

"Is that a fact?" the old gnome asked.

Kris moved slowly with what little aid the gnome was able to give and stepped out into the forest glade. He kept his head low to avoid hitting the tent's low door. Snow had piled up outside with light flurries still coming down. The air bit at his face and hands and he quickly pushed the door closed. Feltahn only laughed as he swiped the cloak from his hands.

They gathered around a fire the gnome had already started. "Not the very top. There lay dangers even I would rather avoid. But one of its peaks." Feltahn wore only a light coat over his clothes but seemed unbothered by the cold.

It was all too much to take in. "How long have I been here?"

Feltahn looked up from fiddling with his hands. "Hmm? Oh, a few days, I think."

"You *think?" What were the others thinking? Did they find Thysilar? Were they still searching for me?*

"I wouldn't worry about them. They've lived far longer than you and know these forests almost as well as me. As for Estelle... she knows you're well." The gnome spoke casually to the point of irritability.

Kris stared at the gnome as he moved on from his fingers to a stick he must have been carving for a while. *How could he have known what I was going to say?* He remembered a few stories about men and women who could control the wild magick of the world. Each time the character met death, but only after causing a hundred more. "What are you?" he whispered.

"A gnome. I thought that was obvious." Feltahn said without sacrificing any attention.

Kris knocked the stick from his hand, his patience wearing thin. "What are you?"

"I was still working on that."

"What are you?"

"A gnome. Or does my appearance bring to mind something else?" Feltahn asked.

"That's not what I meant." Kris said, his anger bleeding into his tone.

"That's hardly a problem of mine. Perhaps you should start meaning what you say. You'll find you waste less of people's time that way." Still the gnome remained calm.

Kris held his fists by his side and elected to clench them tightly instead of knocking the old gnome to the ground, though the thought brought more than a little satisfaction.

"Why did you bother saving me?"

Now Feltahn did look up. "You risked much to save your friend. Someone who has killed many of your people."

"The Falhofnans are –."

"And you stared down a pack of wolves that would have scared off many. Tales of that Alpha are known well around these lands." He shrugged. "Curiosity, I suppose."

"How did you find me?" Kris tried to appear calm. He refrained from mentioning the thicket of roots and branches that bested him.

"Simply enough." the gnome said. "There are a few trees who know their way."

Why can't he just come out and say it? "I was brought to you?"

Feltahn smiled through his beard. "That's what happens when you're sent for."

Kris pushed the tent flap aside as he walked back through and began strapping on his weapons. The armor was worse off than he thought and not worth the extra weight. When he stepped back outside the gnome was back to working at his stick. Feltahn knew more than he was letting on and the fact that he insisted on keeping that information to himself meant he preferred having the upper hand. How could someone like that be trusted? Kris walked towards the edge of the camp where he'd seen a way down from the rise they were on.

"Haven't you ever wondered why she took you in that night?" Feltahn called after him.

He wanted to keep moving, put the gnome and his words behind him. "I was alone in the middle of a snow storm." *Just keep walking.*

"That's why she brought you back. I asked if you knew why she took you in."

As much as he hated to acknowledge it, the gnome had brought up a point Kris thought about more than he liked to admit. Why did she? He was just a human. Thysilar always talked of the things 'his kind' had done to the elves. Their presence was the reason Estelle raised so many children. It took him a moment to notice his legs were still.

"I'm keeping things from you. I'll admit it. They're things I do not plan on keeping forever." He looked up from the carving. "But it would seem I'm not the only one. Trust is something that should be earned. I'm aware of that. In this case, however, I must insist you offer yours regardless."

"Why should I?" Kris asked, unsure why he was still listening.

"Because the trees were mine, like the wolves. And because Estelle decided to take you in and not bargain you off to the next Falhofnan patrol that passed by." The gnome had finally started to sound more serious. "You've already witnessed things today that you thought were not possible, not anymore. Is it too much to ask that you allow me some of that faith?" He tossed the stick into the fire and gazed out over the mountain's edge. In that moment he looked older than before. Gnomes did not share the same exact longevity as the elves, but they surpassed humans by nearly a century. And Feltahn looked to have passed that mark long ago.

Kris was not sure why he decided to stay. He wanted to say that it was because he did not feel well enough to risk the journey back. But there was more. A feeling he could not put words to.

"Unfortunately the best path up the mountain will also take you a week or so around it." Feltahn said. He fed another log to the fire and gestured to the bag leaning against the stump beside Kris. "Eat. Gather your strength. I'd prefer if we left sooner than late."

Neither of them spoke as Kris took his seat by the fire. The brisk air helped keep his head clear. His hands turned over a wooden toy in his pocket, startling him before he realized what it was. How had it gotten there? Estelle told him the stag had been in his cradle the night she found him, tucked beneath the blankets that were wrapped around him. It had been scratched and nicked from play during his younger years, but to him it was perfect. It was a piece of home. Had his mother made it? His father? Did he have any brothers, and if so did they have one just like it? Maybe theirs resembled other animals. He shook his head. *Estelle is my mother, the forest my home.* He repeated the words over, his thumb flicking against the edge of a broken antler.

8

Kris had not been to this area of the forest, but that was to be expected. Aside from his trips with Thysilar he rarely ventured far. The trees had a maleficent quality about them, as though at any moment they might spring to life, dragging the unwary to a deep grave. The leaves were a mix of purples and blues, the colors bleeding down into the bark. A thin layer of frost coated the ground. He scoffed at the wolf skin cloak when the gnome made the offer. It was midsummer, though the seasons seemed to have little meaning this far up the mountain, and the colder months were still a ways off. Feltahn only smiled when Kris pulled it over his shoulders.

For two days and two nights they walked the snow covered ground. Hard as he tried, Kris was unable to keep to the pace. Every hour or so they were forced to stop. Feltahn seemed not to mind, taking the time to read of the handful of books he brought with him. After the fourth day Kris started to doubt the pace set at the outset of their journey did not account for someone slowed by their wounds.

Sweat dripped down his forehead as they reached the top of a steep hill laden with roots and small shrubbery. "Are you alright?" Feltahn asked, passing him the water skin.

Kris drank greedily, pausing to catch his breath. With all the snow around, water was not in short supply. "I could use a rest."

"It'll be night soon anyway. Sit. I'll get a fire started."

They finished what was left of the pork and picked at some of the bread. Kris was given mead sweeter than any he had tried. After the second cup he felt his head swim and drank no more that night. When he woke he was covered with sweat, his limbs weak. Feltahn caught him as he fell to his hands and knees after trying to stand. "Here, drink." He did. "How do you feel?" Feltahn told him to lean back against the tree as he lifted his shirt. "Damn."

Kris tried to look for himself but could not see anything. As far as he knew the dressing on his wounds were fine.

"They're not fine. They're infected. I was hoping I had cleaned them enough but...dammit." Feltahn let the cloth fall back down. "There's a town maybe a day from here. It's been years since I've passed through but it should have someone better suited to mend these than I. Can you make it?"

There was not much of a choice. "I think so."

They could have done without the rain. Kris moved from tree to tree as often as possible, keeping himself balanced. The ground turned soft and treacherous, threatening to trip him up if he was not careful. This became more difficult the longer he remained on his feet. Night came and the storm never wavered. "Stop," Kris said, repeating it louder to be heard over the storm. "I have to stop."

"We can't. The town's not much farther, I promise you." Feltahn said.

Kris moved off the tree he had been leaning on, managing to make it three steps before falling. Water puddled around him. The mud seeped into his rain soaked clothes, but he couldn't feel it. His eyes closed, darkness all around him, still he felt the ground spinning.

9

"Again." the gnome said. Feltahn sat atop a rock with his legs crossed. He held a knotted staff across his lap. "Focus." His eyes remained closed.

Kris sat on the ground with his knees folded. The last few days had seen his strength return, but not fully. He had woken up on a cot with the bodies of stuffed animals mounted along the many shelves surrounding him. His wounds were redressed and his fever had broken. Feltahn gave him a day before putting that strength to the test. He told him the techniques were designed to strengthen his focus while helping his body heal. How the mind could influence such things Kris did not know. *Before this I would not have guessed trees could come to life either.* He promised to show Feltahn a deal of faith, so he would.

Kris glared up at the gnome with a curse on his tongue but held back. Sweat dotted his brow and his body ached from the day's exercise. All were excuses Feltahn wanted nothing to do with. The sooner he felt better the sooner they would leave. He did not know what was waiting for him at the top of the mountain. The question was one the gnome refused to be straight forward about. *He wouldn't have gone through this much trouble if it was not important.* That was all the motivation he needed. He cleared his mind using the technique he had been shown weeks before and waited. Deep breaths filled his lungs before being exhaled. Each was done in rhythm. It had to be perfect.

"What do you see?"

Kris focused his mind, flexing it in the same way he would any other muscle. It was his to control. A powerful tool beyond any other, the gnome had said, "If one knows how to wield it." He reached out but only darkness greeted him. The beginnings of another migraine sprouted behind his eyes. They had become one of the only things he *could* predict. The outline of an image appeared, thin lines being drawn as though from the brush of a painter. His excitement rose and his heart raced. Eagerly he grasped at it, willed it to take full form and present itself to him. Slowly, the phantom took shape. Others joined it, smaller, and just as faint. There was a shimmer of movement between them. Wherever it passed, the lines smudged like wet ink. *Keep going. Almost have it.* He made out the leaves of a bush, the rest of it becoming clear as that truth was revealed. The pain behind his eyes grew.

He spread the knowledge onto the other shrubs and was rewarded with their sudden clarity. A warmth dripped from his nose and he tasted copper. *Can't quit now. I've come too close.* He pushed further and focused his attention on the larger image. He knew what it should be, but his focus was fading. At that thought the other images lost their solidarity. No! He tried to regain the hold he had but the weight of it all was too much. The pain in his head threatened to split through bone and he let go.

The air was cold, stinging as he inhaled. Kris wiped at the blood still pouring from his nose. There was nothing left. Though the last trial dealt with his mental strength and not physical, the exercise proved to put a strain on both. He stared up into the clouded sky and lay there. The gnome would want him to try it again.

Whenever his exhaustion was at its peak, Feltahn pushed him the hardest. This time the image would not be as simple as a few bushes and a tree. *Now why couldn't I see that then as I do now?* How the mind worked differently when he was in reverie was unknown to him. *I guess if it was easy everyone would do it.* He shuddered to think of the trouble that would cause.

"Why did you fail?" Feltahn asked.

"I almost had it." Kris said, "I would have if the headaches didn't start."

The gnome shook his head. "Why did you fail?"

"Because I didn't try hard enough. My focus could use work. I didn't clear my head." The words were well rehearsed and he did his best to say them in the same way Feltahn had. They did nothing but annoy him. He knew why he failed. The headaches made it hard to focus on anything else. But the gnome would hear none of it.

"You failed because you're too distracted. And your temper could use some work." He hopped off the rock and tapped the sole of Kris' boot with the end of his staff. "Get up. That's enough for today."

Thistle Grove was not a large village, tucked away beneath the shadow of the mountain. When Kris was able and walked the length of it he was surprised such a talented healer as Therese chose to live here. She had a small farm at the top of a nearby ridge, kept safe by fences and a few sharpened stakes. Or at least that was her plan. The fences were trampled over closest to the mountain. *Whatever did this was no small beast.* As they entered through the wooden gate of the surrounding palisades they were given the attention of all they passed. Gnomes were not a popular sight to behold in these parts and even further north, where their race was born. But it was not Feltahn the elves were staring at.

"They still don't trust me." Kris said.

"Do they have much reason to?" Feltahn responded. "The last humans they've seen did not come with peace in mind. It's likely they all have friends, family, that were killed in this war. Would you be so forgiving?"

Kris remained silent.

He bathed in the nearby stream, the cold guaranteeing he did not linger long. A storm picked up over the next few days, snow coming down in droves to pile up past his shins. Dinner each night was an array of fruits and bread, with a leg of lamb one night that Kris thought could have used some seasoning. The tavern was one of the few structures left in the village still made entirely of stone. Pelts hung along the walls between a handful of old paintings. More blanketed the floor. Most were bears but a few of the smaller had belonged to wolves. *Large wolves at that.* It was Feltahn who pointed them out as former cloaks. "They used to belong to knights." How they came to hang here Kris did not need to ask. The rest of the patrons gave them a wide berth, preferring to talk and eat amongst themselves. Every few minutes or so a group would pass them a glance and make some comment or another beneath their breath. Hard as it was, Kris ignored them. They sat alone by the fireplace, Kris sipping at his tea, waiting for it to cool.

"You never told me how you came to know Estelle," Kris asked.

The gnome never seemed to have the same problem with his own tea. "It's a long story I'd rather not bore you with."

"That hasn't stopped you before." Kris said with a smirk. Feltahn did not laugh. He remained quiet as he sipped his tea. Kris knew enough of the gnome to sense when to ease away. Rarely had Feltahn opted out of a conversation.

"Mind if I join you?" They both turned to find Therese, plate in one hand and a pint in the other. She was one of the older elves left in the village, her brown hair cut short and graying.

"Of course." Feltahn slid another chair over and she sat.

"I hear the same conversations every night. Fresh faces are not something I care to take for granted." She took a bite of bread and waited to swallow. "What may I ask brings you two this far west of the mountain? It's not often we see either of your races, especially together."

Or without weapons bared, Kris added to himself.

"I'm a writer," Feltahn said, "And a lover of history. I'm working on a new book about the old kingdoms of the mountain, where my people once prospered. He's my assistant."

Therese did not mask her surprise. "Are there many humans in the capital?"

"No," Feltahn said smiling, "Not many. I stumbled across his grandparents on my way to the coast. They have been in my employ and friendship ever since."

Kris sipped at his tea and hoped his curiosity did not give away the ruse.

"That was very kind of you, gnome. Unfortunately I cannot say they would have received the same treatment here." Therese said. "If it was not me you came to it is likely your friend would have been left to die."

The eyes around them seemed suddenly hostile. "Has there been much fighting here? I noticed the damage to your fence and wall." Feltahn turned to him but Kris ignored it.

"No. It's been a long while since any Falhofnans ventured this far."

"It could not have been a storm." Kris said plainly. The damage was too direct.

"It was something else." Therese said, "Something we've learned to fear more."

When she did not say more, Kris pushed further. "What, then? Raiders? Pirates?" He had heard stories of those elves whose own homes were lost so they lived by preying on their own, stealing and killing to survive.

"Enough." Feltahn said, his voice stern. "If she does not wish to say –."

"No, it's alright." Therese said. "It's a frost troll, from somewhere along the mountain. Where it's made its home, we've not been able to find out."

"A yeti…" Feltahn said more to himself than anyone else.

"Have you sent men to search for it?" Kris asked. He heard a few tales from elven soldiers fortunate enough to have survived encounters with them. As tall as an oak with limbs half as thick, it was no wonder the people here were in such dire straits.

"Many. But the dead can say nothing." Therese looked away, sipping slowly at her ale.

"I'm sorry. I didn't mean –."

"No, of course not." An elf said, rising from his table nearby. "None of you ever mean the things you do. Blameless, you are. Is that what you'd like us to believe?"

Therese moved to stand between Kris and the elf. "Sit down, Walther."

"I think I've sat long enough." Walther responded. Kris could smell the ale on his breath. "If it was not for his kind we could have sent for aid. Let the Red Cloaks put this beast down and be done with it. Roland, Edwin…Mariele."

"We've all lost someone." Therese said softly. "The last thing we need is more bloodshed."

Kris sat still as stone. Walther stared at him without a word for what felt like hours before taking the cup from Therese's hand and finishing what was left inside before returning to his seat.

"I'm sorry about that." Therese said. "His wife was killed during the first of the raids. His sons were part of the group that went out to hunt it."

"It's alright." Kris said, his voice faint, his eyes distant.

Sleep eluded him. He lay awake on his bed until he could no longer stand it. The fire had died down and taken most of the heat with it. He wrapped the fur cloak around himself. Walther's words repeated themselves over in his mind. Kris could not rid himself of the elf's face. His grief. *He blames me. All of them do. Why shouldn't they? If it wasn't for my people coming here so much would be different. Maybe his family would still be alive. Maybe...* He shut his eyes and silenced himself. He could not be in his own mind tonight. Feltahn had brought books, after all. It had been too long since Kris read.

Kris hovered just outside his door and waited. The snoring continued for minutes more before he was convinced the gnome was very much asleep. He was cautious with the door, figuring when it would squeak and how best to avoid it. The gnome's bed was not scaled to meet his size and Feltahn looked like a child on the oversized mattress. The room was built like a mirror to his own, with the bed against the wall away from the door and a small dresser to his right. The bedside table was just a few feet from him. He walked softly on bare feet, crouching down to get a better grip on the handle of the drawer. It slid free with relative ease and did not make a sound. Inside he found what he was looking for. Feltahn kept a journal that Kris remembered seeing him writing in. The gnome likely thought he did so without notice. Kris never stared for long but he knew enough to guess those pages would hold at least something pertaining to the real reason Feltahn was so interested in him. And it was not the only book there. Another, older tome rested half-covered beneath it. The lettering on the worn out leather was faded. The indentation, however, Kris could still make out.

It was a stag.

Kris fed another log to the fire and opened the hard-covered book. He should not have been surprised to find the handwriting near-impossible to decipher. *I would've preferred it to be written in code. He writes in more riddles than he speaks.* It took some getting used to but eventually his eyes adjusted to some of the little nuances Feltahn used while writing. What little he managed to decode was senseless, nothing but the mind's rambling given form on paper. He sat there by the fire until it had eaten most of the wood before deciding there was no use in continuing.

Feeling more defeated than before, he took up the thicker volume. The spine cracked as he opened it. The pages were aged, the ink not lasting in some places. It was a history text. Falhofnan. Kris thumbed his way through a few chapters, most of them dealing with dead kings he never knew or heard of, and was ready to give up on this one as well when an image caught his eye. It was another stag, this one resembling the one stitched on the blanket still in his room back at Estelle's cabin. What's this? He thought. "Niklas and Katja Dobryn," he said aloud. It was easier for him to think this way. "Third of his House. No siblings. Inherited the Barony from his father Andre. They were the family to take up the title once the last of the Kalugs finally died out." They had one child. It said nothing else about them, other than their death and the succession of Baron Gerold.

Kris flipped back and forth from the last page and the one after it as though if he did it fast enough the answers would suddenly appear to him, having been there all along. That did not turn out to be the case.

He returned both books to their place in the drawer, unable to fight the feeling in his chest. Feltahn would have answers. Kris would be sure they were given this time. He was ready to close the drawer when he noticed something else. There were scraps of loose pages piled in no discernible order covering what appeared to be the corner to a picture frame. He brushed the paper aside and gently pulled it free.

The painting was bordered with grey wood, the image inside showing no signs of the age that affected its frame. Beautiful was not a strong enough word to describe the woman granted immortality through ink. There was no doubt she was an elf. Every line of her face, each dimple, was given hours of attention. Her smile disarmed. Her eyes stared straight through, taking away what armor he had left. A single rose of deep violet adorned the curls of her auburn hair. *An old lover? A wife?* Whoever she was, for whatever reason she was no longer a part of his life. Kris' gaze drifted over to the old gnome, filtered with a newborn melancholy. Feltahn shifted in his sleep and he left as quickly as he had come.

His head felt swollen and another migraine was well on the way.

Kris woke to the smell of bacon. His body ached, finding little rest throughout the night. That did not bode well. Today was like to be just as exhaustive. They ate their breakfast in silence. Feltahn waited as Kris dressed himself for another day spent out in the thin, cold air. He waited until Kris finished moving through the first stations of the swordplay technique he had been teaching him before addressing the uncommon quiet. "What troubles you?"

Kris did not try to hide it. He had done that enough. "You know so much about me, my childhood, yet you give nothing up about yourself."

"What is it you'd like to know?"

Just days ago, Kris would have latched onto those words and not let go, so enthralled would he have been with the promise of answers. "You ask me that but I know you'll say nothing." He continued his footwork and followed through with the motion perfectly. It was not a style he was familiar with, though it was influenced in part by what he saw Thysilar use. Swordplay was his stronger field but even so it left much to be desired. Even that was vexing. *What does it matter?* Kris finished the imaginary opponent and stabbed the invisible sword into the hard-packed earth. "What's next?"

They went through the warm ups trying to get Kris' mind clear and ready. He was able to get an extra shrub farther before falling to the ground. "Again." Feltahn said. And so they began anew. Kris had been expecting the same forest scene and when it did not come he felt his anger boil over. "What are you doing?" the gnome asked as Kris walked to the edge of the clearing. "We're not finished."

"Doing what, exactly? How does this help me do…whatever the gods only know what you're trying to prepare me for?" The words came unhindered and without forethought.

"As I told you before, if you wish to help your friends win this war you will need to learn things they cannot teach you. I can. Now clear your mind."

Kris ignored him, remaining where he stood. "Why should I believe you? If you have the power you claim then why have you waited all these years? How many other stories like this village took place throughout the forest? Did you take pleasure in watching the number of deaths rise?" He knew what he said was harsh but at that moment he did not care.

Feltahn opened his eyes from where he sat and Kris could have sworn he saw frost glaze over them. "You know nothing, boy. Don't pretend to lecture me about loss."

"Who was she?" He had hoped to save the picture for a better moment but he was asking the question before his mind could think and take it back.

His eyes betrayed his response. "Who?"

There's no backing away now. "The woman in the picture. Who was she?"

Feltahn took his weight off of the staff. His long breaths steamed in the cold. "You went through my things."

"As you went through my head."

"You went through my things." Feltahn said again.

"You gave me no choice." Kris was feeling less confident but dared not back down now. "How else would I get any straight answers?"

The gnome seemed to consider the thought, but not for long. "Leave."

"What?" Kris asked, his shock plain on his face.

"I said leave. You were right. There are others I can instruct. Others better suited and more mature." Feltahn turned his back on Kris and walked without need of his staff. "The path home will reveal itself."

Kris stared into the falling snow as Feltahn disappeared within the trees, half expecting him to emerge from behind a rock, saying how he had passed some test. He was not sure how long he stood there before realizing that would not be the case.

10

Torches sputtered as a cool wind passed, the flames dancing as their shadows twisted and warped. Gerold's knees ached from staying so long on the hard stone floor. In front of him stood Abelard, the first king of all men, one hand on the haft of his axe while the other rested on the head of a bear unequaled in size. Both were carved from marble and smoothed over until they rivaled those in the church at the capital. The only armor he wore was boiled leather and fur with his head bare and exposed, daring an enemy to strike. *Let the shepherd meet the warrior in battle. This is the face of a true god.* Conversion had increased as more such churches were torn down or left to rot. *Let them go. Only the weak are swayed by sly words. The strong still remain.* Abelard, Lord of the Earth, was not known to forget.

Gerold touched his hand to the bear emblem on his shirt and then to the statue, his prayer ended. He was never particularly religious. His father was killed avoiding his gambling debts and his mother, as hard as she tried, which he always gave her credit for, could not handle the pressure of the times. Alcohol took her. Being alone for so long taught Gerold many things, but none more important than the reliance on himself. No one was going to give him things in this world. If he wanted to survive he would have to do so on the strength of his own will. It saw him rise from a beggar on the streets to a general in the Falhofnan army. It was that fact that whispered to him when Niklas first started his anti-war musings. The king wanted the elves' power to forever deal with his rivals in the east. How would he do so without this war? All he needed was royal support, a promise that the executioner won't be coming for his head, and the coup was set in motion. All of this was done by his will. Not prayer. The priest came over to him robed in furs of brown and black. A bear's head rested over his shoulder, its dead eyes staring into the baron. *But the people treasure their religion.* He bowed slightly. *And who am I if not a man of the people?* Most of their brotherhood allowed their facial hair to grow freely in homage to their patron, but not all took it as seriously as the priest, Bern. The braids of both his hair and beard, while much greyer than when he was first given the position, reached nearly to his waist and looked to be growing still. "My Lord." The baron nodded his head and motioned for Bern to rise. "May I ask what troubles you at this late hour?"

"I prefer to speak my prayers alone, Brother. Less chance they'll be mixed in with the rest."

"All are heard here."

"Yes, but are all listened to?" Gerold's smile disarmed the priest. "But I did not come here to discuss theology. Only a blessing, with hopes that this war will soon end."

"Of course, my lord. These elves worship air and dirt. The Great Bear will tread over them with ease and leave the bones to bleach." Bern was sure in his convictions and did not waver. The words were taken almost directly from scripture.

They worship more than just air and dirt. And once it's mine, my place here will be solidified. He fought for everything ever since he was a child in the streets of Dhal. Nothing would be given to him.

Everything he had was earned. Or taken. This was no different. Blood and sweat were his currency, and in that regard he was wealthy. "I trust you'll add your prayers to see that it does." Gerold left, pulling his hood up over his head as he went. He had left his guards back at the keep. The streets had grown dangerous with the tax increase as some people began taking to less legal means of making a living. They were growing desperate, but so was he. He patted the pommel of his sword, reassured by its weight.

The streets were empty save for the occasional drunk stumbling his way home. One tried to talk his way into getting a better look at the sword while another fancied the cloak draped over his shoulders. All they received were broken bones. No one bothered him the rest of the walk. Gerold made his way into the western end of the city and kept his hand not far from his blade. Anyone who wanted something from him here would not waste time with words. Babes cried out of open windows sparsely lit from flickering candles. The ground underneath was wet and caused his boots to sink. He kept his eyes straight, his stride confident. The men here would prey on weakness. *I am the baron and descendant of the Bear.*

The walk back seemed longer than before. He should have felt relieved.

He entered the keep through the hidden passage he was less than pleased to learn existed during the first year of his rule. The man who brought it to his attention would not be telling another. He hung his cloak on the post by his bed, changing into a soft wool robe and opening the window to the cooler air. There was no one voice in his mind, but a chorus, all speaking the same words together. Gerold poured a glass of wine from the pitcher he had brought before he left, drank it down, and then refilled it. Few else could quell their persistence. He stared out to the mountain and the forest surrounding it. There had been no word of Anton. Nearly a month, yet nothing. He refused to believe it when the whispers told him his favored scout was dead, his body joining the dozens of others that fell doing just what he intended. *The cost of this quest is even greater than I feared.* But he would pay it. Even if that meant the life of a man who's served more loyally than any other in his city.

The baron sipped at his wine, his gaze sweeping across to the west, toward the capital.

11

Estelle always hated being at court. Her mother sat in a chair fit for a queen, the wood grown naturally with the branches forming to fit her body perfectly. A dress of coral adorned her slim figure, matching the crown of roses that rested on her brow. There were no lines on her face though by all rights there should have been. She conveyed confidence in front of the other nobles sitting around the table. Only Estelle could see the worry behind her mother's eyes.

There were six others present with only two missing. Some wore fineries akin to the queen's while others opted for less flashy clothing. Two in particular caught Estelle's attention. She had seen soldiers before but did not expect to see them present at such gatherings. When she brought it up to her mother she was given a smile and told that Maia and her brother Danilo were from a region closer to the mountain and raised accordingly. They did not have the luxury of safety from the many dangerous beasts as the elves deeper in the forest had. She spoke of them with respect but all Estelle saw was roughness. *It's a wonder they are not home gathering for some sort of attack.* The humans were continuing to keep them at a distance with trades and as their payments grew later and later it would only be a matter of time until a limit was reached. And then....War was something she only knew of in stories.

"And what would you have us do?" El' Nir asked. He was a tall elf and thin, with wisps of white hair braided behind his head.

"Something," Maia said, "Anything is better than letting these humans walk over us like this." She was one of the elves from the mountains and looked the part. Her hair was shorter and tied up allowing her rugged face to be open to all. It's unfortunate, Estelle thought. *She could truly look beautiful if she gave it any effort.* A quiver of arrows was slung across her back, over her cloak.

"Violence cannot be the answer here," one noble said.

"Sometimes we are left with no other choice," another chimed in.

El' Nir was not willing to back away so easily, addressing his next words towards the queen. "Their race is still young. We should guide them towards the right path."

Queen Azaera listened without reaction. Though her rule was long – nearly four centuries – she had yet to be truly tested in this way. There was the frost troll incursion a few decades ago, but they were just beasts. No real strategy was required, at least not by her. That was what the military was for. *One had to take in all sides with equal attention should a fair judgment be made.* Her mother's words echoed in her head as she watched the gathered shift in their seats. Whatever she decided here would resonate throughout the forest. "Commander Danilo, you've been unusually quiet. What are your opinions on the matter?"

"He and Maia are of the same blood; of course he will side with her," El' Nir said.

The queen only cast a glance and the elf was silenced.

Danilo sat beside Maia and but for the light beard that he wore he would have been nearly identical to his twin. "The humans are insulting us with their actions. If we simply sit by and let them continue we will appear weak."

El' Nir sighed and appeared to accept defeat.

"But war may prove even more costly. We do not have the numbers to meet them on the open fields and their castle will withstand all but the mightiest of our siege crafts. As it is we would have to cut down much to supply our woodsmen for the task."

"My queen, I have already said as much to this council a dozen –." El' Nir was cut off as Azaera raised her hand. Not being allowed to speak grated at him.

Seeing that he was not going to be interrupted again Danilo continued. "Until we have proof that their supplies are not in fact being lost to the forest it will be difficult to rally the others to fight. Allow me and my scouts to track the next one."

Queen Azaera considered the idea in silence for what Estelle felt to be longer than necessary. The other councilors showed no signs of sharing her displeasure. After a while Azaera looked up from the emerald set into a ring on her finger. "You must not be seen."

Danilo smiled, the action not one Estelle thought the elf had much practice with. "We will be as shadows, my queen."

The rest of the meeting went by without much excitement. One noble, a woman with hair the color of fire, made a case for expanding her governed territory by claiming a nest of apes native to the forest takes up nearly half of it. Another blamed the increasing lack of trade on losing too much in the lost shipments offered to the Falhofnans. "I was promised double my offerings in return before their column was 'lost'." The queen handled each with respect but Estelle saw that she was growing tired of their issues. By dusk the council had concluded and the nobles dismissed. Maia and Danilo were the first out of the hall and wasted no time exchanging pleasantries as the others did. Estelle was forced to wait until the last said their farewell before she too was allowed to leave.

The hall was built millennia ago when magick still flowed through her people. Alike to the rest of the city its structure was formed seamlessly, mirroring the trees that surrounded it. Autumn was approaching as the leaves and other foliage that draped over it had already started to take on shades of orange and bronze. Weirlights shone from the branches above. There were no soldiers on the ground but Estelle knew they were there. None would pass within a hundred yards without notice. Her mother was going to remain with her advisors a while longer. The escort was waiting by a horse-drawn carriage but she did not join them. It was a nice night, one of the last before winter came. She was set on enjoying it.

Her mobility was limited in the dress she wore. She reached down to the slit already in the hem meant to not completely restrict her movement and tore it up even further. Lady Sehor would not have approved at the amount of skin she showed. *I can almost imagine her face.* The things that woman did not know about her. About him. The thought caused her to smile. All around the forest was alive. The wind blew a light breeze at her back and brought with it the scent of pine. There was a moistness in the air preceding a storm to come. She always loved that smell.

Thunder boomed in the distance and brought Estelle out of her dream. She lay on the couch for moments more as the feelings still lingered in her mind and chest. *Where had that come from?* The fire had dwindled and the air grown cold. She pulled the blanket down from the back cushion and wrapped it around herself as she walked to the icebox for a drink. How late into the night it was Estelle did not know but she had had her fill of sleep.

The candle in her hand shed just enough light to see by, though she trusted her memory and over a century of living in this cabin to be able to find her way in the blackest of nights. A small bookshelf that just reached her hip stood against the wall opposite her bed. There were not many books but each was a favorite, well-read and worn. She was reminded of the great library at Sol' Lian. The capital city was vast. Built into the massive trees that took root so deep into the forest, it was the first settlement their people built. The perfect example of the beauty that their alliance with the magical forces of the world could bring. And a reminder of what they lost. How many hours had she spent there, surrounded by thousands of books and scrolls? How many sleepless nights? *And how many times did he join me? How many promises broken?* Estelle took up a collection of stories she used to read to her children and fed another log to the fire.

She flipped through the pages with no true aim. Each story had been read dozens upon dozens of times. There were old favorites, some she preferred less than others, but none that she truly disliked. Her thumb stopped at the title page to the second-to-last tale. *The Winter Wizard.* Estelle remembered when the story was first written and had even dined with the author when Throara was invited to the queen's table. Her mother had a soft spot for writers and artists. The book followed a young elf from long ago, when magick was still alive. He was pursued and sought after by all the lords and ladies, bandits and mercenaries of the north. Scholars wished to use him with hopes of bringing magick back. None could find him. It was said that his spirit still haunted the caves and darker places of the forest, 'eager to claim the unwary.' The words had lost much of their luster since she first read them. The truth tended to do that. *She had a lot right, but not him.* There were hundreds of stories floating from town to town and it was Throara who began to piece them together. Who could say how much more she would have unearthed if the Falhofnans had not hit the traders she was traveling with. *Who could say?* She had gone down the 'what if' road too many times before and did not have the patience for such a trip again. The book closed louder than she intended, amplified by the quiet all around her.

That was the one thing she had never fully gotten used to. The sounds of so many children living under the same roof, as unpleasant as most would find it, calmed her, becoming like one of the lullabies her grandmother would sing to help her sleep. There were moments in between where the house was left to her but this was the first where she was forced to acknowledge that this time it was like to last longer. *Unless the war takes yet another turn.* She had remained beyond the lines of conflict but the Falhofnans would not be held forever. *Listen to me, resigning to defeat. Wouldn't father be proud?*

A flash of lightning illuminated all in a pale blue light. Estelle opened the window in her bedroom and lay down. The rain would start soon.

12

He was told the path would reveal itself, but not which to take. *I should have guessed it was another damn riddle.* That path could wait. Right now he had another to take. Therese was not specific on where that first party had gone in search of the Yeti. In truth she tried to keep him from going. "You don't need to do this." She didn't understand. How could she? Walther proved more helpful. *It was almost as though the elf wanted me to go to my death.* Kris smiled at that and pushed aside a few low branches as he kept moving. The path was becoming harder to follow. *If only the gnome spent some time teaching me to track.* Thysilar and the others had tried but their lessons never took.

As the sun continued to move across the sky he spent more time thinking over Feltahn's first words to him that night by the fire. He was ready to leave then but could not refuse the questions planted in his mind. Was Estelle keeping things from him as well? If so then what were they? She would not go through the effort of raising a human for over twenty years if she did not care about him. *Why* Estelle took him in that night was unimportant. She loved him as he did her. Like family. Then why was Kris unable to ignore that there was a measure of truth to the gnome's words?

The ground ended abruptly and Kris nearly slipped, so deep in thought. His arm reached out for a nearby tree and gripped a branch. It tensed with his weight but did not break. He steadied his nerves and took a few steps back. The greens of treetops filled his vision, covering the ground beneath him like a cushion, promising comfort should he fall. *Right. The other way, then.*

It had grown dark, the moon hidden behind layers of clouds. Rain came pouring down. Trudging through the storm for hours left his clothes soaked all the way through. A dull ache started to spread throughout his legs. He needed to find shelter. Even with the day's walking he was still on the mountain, though he had stayed more towards the edge hoping to find a faster way down. There were piles of stone here and there that had fallen from the bulk of the mountain but nothing substantial or with enough cover to keep him dry. *A place from the wind would be nice. Might be able to get a fire going.* The weather was nothing if unpredictable. And if he hoped to make it through this night he would need to do so dry. *Who knew how many more there would be?* After another hour of searching he spotted a cave with a mouth taller and wider than himself. He could not pass it up.

Kris kept a hand to the wall as he entered so he would not get turned around. There was no light here and who knew what could be waiting in the shadows. He was silent, listening. The wind blew stronger outside, muffling the raindrops. He heard the sound of his own breathing, heavy and labored. Nothing from further down. *There's that, at least.* The lack of light meant the only way he could know for sure just how deep it went was to continue down until he reached the end. He looked back at the mouth, the water coming down harder than before and at a slant, and decided it was safe enough. His aching limbs did not disagree.

He packed a few bits of food and filled his water skin before he left, taking a few sips as he took out a piece of hard bread. A few twigs and dry leaves had been blown inside but not enough to burn for long. Kris lingered along the edge of the cave mouth, gathering all that he could before piling them away from the storm. He struck a small spark into life and blew lightly to get the rest to catch. The light it provided showed more tinder lying further back. He sat with his back to the wall as he ate, the outer layer of his clothes lying by the fire to dry. He was not sure when he drifted off, but the sound that woke him did not come from the storm.

Kris slowly notched an arrow to his bow, moving with caution in hopes he would avoid drawing any avoidable hostility. The sound could have been a wolf, and if so there was more than one. It was the silent ones he would have to worry about. His sword was loose in its sheath. *Fire and draw.* He had the cliff at his back. There would be nowhere to run. A sound like stone dragged across the floor, getting nearer. The fire burned low, having gone unfed, and cast ghostly shadows in the orange light. Kris kept his breathing minimal. His aim was steady. The noise travelled along the stone and made it difficult for him to tell just how close whatever it was he had disturbed was getting. The waiting tested his patience. When at last the figure emerged from the darkness he cursed for his luck.

The beast was apelike in appearance but there the comparison ended. It stood at least eight feet tall, white fur covering it from head to toe. The flesh around its eyes was pale blue, the same found on the palms of its hands and the soles of its feet. Years had turned them to leather, strong and durable where the winter was harshest. A thicket of sharp teeth crisscrossed from its mouth, and more than a few stuck out, poking at the beast's lips. In its hand it held what Kris assumed to be the trunk of a small tree, a boulder tied to its end with strands of hair. Kris was frozen in place at the sight. He felt his chances, slim as they had been, slip away with the wind. The beast stopped a dozen feet from him, the fire between them, and stared.

He had an opportunity to strike while it appeared to be unawares but stayed his hand. *It hasn't attacked yet. Might be it'll return without a fight.* No sooner had he spoken the words to himself than the yeti opened its maw and howled. Kris nearly dropped his bow to shield his ears. Bits of meat still clung to its teeth. The club moved with a speed betrayed by its apparent weight and Kris tossed himself against the wall to avoid being caught beneath it. His arrow slipped, the shot going wide to clatter harmlessly against the stone. The beast was angry at having missed and shifted its weight to send another strike. Again Kris threw himself from the blow, diving into a roll. His hand found the hilt of his sword and the steel sang as it was drawn. The fire flickered as the wind changed course. Drops of rain hit his back. The beast was forced to crouch as the ceiling narrowed, its yellow eyes not once leaving him. The fire whispered its final breath as a large foot smothered it.

Darkness returned and claimed much of the beast with it. Seeing no other choice Kris backed out of the cave and into the wind and the rain where there was still some light to be had. The clouds thinned for a moment, allowing some of the moonlight to shine down. He should run, he knew, but where? The storm had not ceased and the night was only getting colder. With no supplies or warmer clothes he would not last another day. The beast stepped outside and grinned. "Your mistake." Kris said before doing the first thing that came to mind and charged.

The club swung down inches to his left, sending clumps of dirt to the air to shower down on him. It howled its displeasure and went to lift its weapon for a second try. Kris did not give it the chance. His sword sliced deep into its forearm, requiring effort to dislodge. The large weapon dropped from loose fingers as another sound erupted from the beast's lips. This time it was pain. It clutched at the wound with its other hand, kicking out at Kris before he could follow up with another strike. The yeti did not linger long on the cut. It roared, lunging out with its fist. Kris dropped out of the way as the blow connected with a tree, splintering the wood. He got to his feet as it stomped down. He was getting lucky, he knew. *But luck won't last forever.*

Unable to make a fist, the beast swung its wounded arm like that of a rag doll. Kris hopped back but not far enough. The blow clipped him in the ribs, sending him spinning to crash into the rock of the mountain. He felt the air leave his lungs and he gasped, desperately trying to get it back. His sword slipped from his grasp. A ringing started in his ears and refused to stop. *Get up. You can't lay here.* The beast would not let an opening like this go. Kris managed to roll onto his back but nothing else. He thought of Estelle and the cabin, Thysilar and the others. *Will they know what happened? Will Feltahn find me? Will he care?* He closed his eyes to the blue and white mass rushing toward him.

When he opened them again Kris was staring up at the bottom of a big blue foot. It should have crushed him. It should have ground him into the dirt so deep that no power left to the world could unearth him. But it hadn't. His vision regained focus. The clearer the image became the less sense it made. Thick roots from a nearby oak had the limb pinned against the side of the mountain. The beast grasped at it, pulling and picking and when that did not work it brought its fists down over and over. It gnashed its teeth and howled. The roots moved then, shifting like a serpent and sending the beast crashing down. The ground shook.

Another figure, smaller, stepped by Kris' side. "Get up." His voice was familiar but Kris could not quite place it. He felt his mind put itself back together with a fresh speed not his own. "I said up. It will not stay down for long."

Kris did as he was told and only on his feet did his mind serve him fully once more. "Feltahn?"

The old gnome looked as he always had, yet different somehow. He held no staff to support him and moved with an energy reserved for the young. His eyes appeared to glow an icy blue. "Stay behind. I would rather not have to worry about you as well." Feltahn turned back toward the yeti and gestured his hand forward. The roots reacted as they were bid, coiling up and ready to strike. They held back, however. The beast rose angrier than it had been since the fight began. It had no idea it had already lost.

Feltahn twisted his other hand. The ground beneath the yeti's feet loosened, the mud pulling it down up to its knees. Panic seized the beast as it pummeled the dirt. Chunks of soil and rock flew all around but before it made any real progress the roots struck. Lines of red opened up along its arms and chest, stark against the white of its hide. It brought its arms protectively over its face only to have them torn and slashed nearly to shreds. With its last remnants of strength it pulled itself free from the ground and lashed out at the roots.

The gnome was unfazed. *How could he have hid this power from me?* Kris wanted to be angry, to scorn Feltahn for keeping a secret such as this. What were illusionary parlor tricks compared to commanding the very earth? He stepped back as the giant's stare was fixed on Feltahn. He kept his calm. The yeti howled as it ran, its arm raised over its head. Kris moved to pull the gnome out of the way when the mountain cracked. A stone nearly the size of the beast itself tore free and rushed into its side. There was no howl, no cry, only a short yelp before it was knocked over the ledge. Kris rushed to the cliff as the tops of the trees below buckled and cracked under the weight. Feltahn came to stand beside him. "I told you to go back. Why did you come here?"

"You heard Walther. How could I not?"

The gnome's eyes faded back to their original shade. "And yet you ask why I sent for you."

Unable to think of better words, Kris asked, "Is it dead?"

"It's safe to say." A smile crossed his face, amusement to a joke only he knew. "Unless these beasts can bounce."

II

1

The man made no sound when he died. He tried, but only blood escaped his lips. It did not take long until his eyes glazed over, staring. The Red Cloak pulled his spear from the Falhofnan's throat and moved on to the next. Thysilar stood by their own dead, rubbing at the ache in his shoulder. His wounds had been slow to heal over the past year. *How many did this make now? Seventy? Eighty?* He had been promoted after the raid of the Falhofnan camp and while he tried convincing the others that all he did was get more elves killed, they insisted he accept. So he did. Instead of making suggestions he gave orders. *The results remained the same.* He was given more soldiers and assigned targets every few weeks or so, but other than that, he was allowed freedom to act however he wished. Today it was a supply column transporting food from the nearby farms.

The farms were liberated after the food was taken, the elves there regrouping with the rest of Thysilar's company for the main strike. It was perfect on paper. *But battles are not fought with words or in the mind. They're fought here.* The bodies beneath their red cloaks were more reminders of that. No matter how well-planned a strategy was, there were always variables. Things that could not be accounted for. *Their families will not care about the details of combat. All they'll see is the pale flesh and still limbs, knowing it was on my orders that they fell.* He was told not to let such things linger. "They will only poison your mind and weaken your wits," Maia had said. It was easy enough to hear, but something altogether different once the sounds of fighting dwindled. *The Butcher's Bill. A fitting name.*

"Sir," one of his Red Cloaks said, nodding his head slightly. "We've rounded up the few who ran off. They were heading for The Pine Fort."

The Falhofnans had three true fortifications in the forest to advance their lines and keep pressure on the elves. Two were all but abandoned and left with a skeleton crew as they continued their push. The furthest was The Pine Fort. Thysilar heard other elves call it that, claiming the name originated from the amount of pine trees they had cut to see it built. He was glad those men were caught. The Pine Fort held the largest garrison in the area. And they had just denied them their next months' worth of food. *We'll let them starve for a while.* "Well done, Caeldeth. Once the supplies are moved put the bodies in. The Falhofnans will want to know what's keeping their wagons."

Caeldeth smiled, looping his bow over his shoulder. "Very good, sir." The elf was irreplaceable during Thysilar's first months in command.

They marched back to camp more talkative than before. The threat of death and battle was no longer so prevalent. *Let them enjoy today. Tomorrow is no guarantee.* Thysilar walked at the head of the column and went over a letter sent by bird earlier this morning. His orders had been arriving more frequently the last few months in what he assumed was preparation for something larger. Each supply line he severed, every patrol and outpost he ambushed was acting under Commander Berengar. And Commander Berengar held The Pine Fort. "She means to take it." Thysilar whispered. Was she mad? Maia used bold tactics in the past, but nothing like this. There were not enough elves in the area to lay a proper siege and even if there were the task would prove costly. The Falhofnans knew more of such warfare than the elves ever would. "We'd be playing into their hands."

Thysilar hung his armor on the stand by his cot and sat at his desk. The table was small and easy to move with their constant moving but was not too uncomfortable. On it lie the dozen or so letters Maia had sent him over the year since his promotion. Five had been from the last four months. *And this makes six*. He added the most recent to the pile and sipped at his honeyed wine. It was overly sweet but strong enough so that he did not mind for long.

The map before him detailed the area of the forest he was given governance over. Thysilar made room as he unfolded another, this one showing the whole of the Elven Kingdom. Maia led their largest force and had seen the most victories. Her people were bred hard by the mountain, strong. He had had the chance to fight with them only once but it was enough to showcase their combat prowess. "I've hunted many beasts but never a bear so skinny." he remembered one of them saying. She would be further north, repelling the Falhofnans burning along the mountain's base. Aelen, commander of the Eastern armies, would be leading his Red Cloaks through the Eastwood to engage the army currently burning half of it down. No one had heard from Sylvara. It was likely the west already fell with her. *Berengar likely has her head at his gate*. She would not have been the first to meet such an end. The Bear enjoyed his trophies.

Thysilar traced the outline of his camp's movement with his finger. The medical supplies by Tier'Nahl. A mounted patrol along the Ivy River. He was not surprised to find his finger moving closer and closer to The Pine Fort. The next order continued with that trend. *In a month she'll have me at the walls with nothing but ladders to take them*. He swallowed another draught of wine. The noise outside his tent was faint, only a few conversations heard over the crackling fires and chirping crickets. Over three hundred elves once occupied this camp, filling the night with cheerful laughter and song after a good day. Barely half that number remained. He could not remember the last time he heard any music.

The tent flaps were pushed aside as Caeldeth entered, unarmored but wearing his cloak. "May I have a word, sir?"

Thysilar pushed the papers aside and gestured for him to sit down. "Drink?"

"No, sir. Thank you." Caeldeth was not the type to hold his tongue yet now he sat in silence, as though trying to find the right way to begin.

"There's no reason to worry over words here. Speak your mind."

"I only say this because I consider ourselves to be friends. There's been talk amongst the others." He was reluctant to continue but Thysilar urged him on. "There's talk that you're being too reckless and it's their blood being paid for it. They say more have died since you took command. It was light at first but it seems more have been inclined to agree."

Thysilar wanted to say how he is only following orders, same as they are. He wanted to walk up to each elf speaking about him and shout it to their faces where they lack the courage. But he remained still, silent. He already lacked the respect of his soldiers. Neither of those choices would help get it back. The next victory needed to be absolute. "Maybe we need a little recklessness."

"Sir?" Caeldeth asked, but by then Thysilar had left the tent.

He did not sleep well but chalked it up to the wine. It rarely agreed with him. Their scouts moved above from tree to tree, unseen by any but those of equal training. Thysilar envied them. It had been too long since he took up his bow. The branches were treacherous, he remembered. *How many times had I nearly fallen, reaching for a branch not as strong as it first appeared?* He was not afraid to stare down an enemy with good steel in hand, but he could not deny the sense of power he felt stalking his prey, his presence masked only until death was a certainty. That life was behind him now. He had moved on to bigger game.

Caeldeth would be up there, he knew. There was no one better with a bow. He was the only one to approach him after his speech at the camp. "I won't say that helped with your 'reckless' image, but I think most got the point. There are not many who enjoy having their oaths called into question."

"I wish it could've gone another way. But such talk can't be tolerated." Thysilar had responded.

"No. That it cannot." They had both been too preoccupied with the march over the next few days but Thysilar did not need his insight to see that the mood of his soldiers had changed. Whether for better or ill he did not know.

The air was damp when they started the march, carrying with it a chill Thysilar was not happy to feel. The last winter had been harsh and its hold was still felt, though not as intensely. They were maybe a day or two from the pass. *If I'm lucky we'll get there in time for another of Maia's birds to arrive, this one telling me to take The Pine. The others would love me then.* He was not sure how her hawks managed to know where he was and when he would be there but they did. *Maybe there is still some magick left in this world.*

He had not talked of what he saw in the forest with anyone aside from Estelle. It was not that Thysilar feared for his reputation. There were those who still held out hope that magick would return to their race. He was not one of them. What he saw, how real it looked... he wanted to believe it. So much so that he surprised himself. Magick meant hope. With it, they could drive the humans out of the forest in months and ensure they would never return. They would bring these invaders to their knees much as they had their own people in the wars before. *And that is why it will remain lost. It knows that only death would follow its return. We had our chance.* He felt his mood sour with the thought.

A shout brought his attention towards the back of their column. More followed it. Thysilar pushed his way past those moving too slow when an arrow brushed past his ear, drawing a line of blood before embedding itself in the chest of the elf behind him. "Cover! Ambush!" He ducked behind a nearby tree and drew his blade. Those that heard him did the same, notching arrows to return fire.

How could they have been caught so unaware? They had scouts all around to keep this sort of thing from happening. Two more arrows thudded into the tree. Thysilar scanned the treetops above for any sign of who may have loosed them. He thought he saw a shadow beyond the leaves but could not be sure. "Pyor, fire there." Thysilar pointed to make sure she knew where he meant. She did. The arrow found its mark, the Falhofnan falling to the ground after hitting a few branches on the way down.

Thysilar risked exposure and ran from his cover to crouch down by the fallen soldier. He was dressed in armor uncommon for Falhofnan scouts, the boiled leather and cloths dyed to blend into the forest seamlessly. Thysilar had to admit he was impressed. He had no bear insignia but instead bore the head of a hawk on his shoulder. A composite bow lay inches from his open hand. Thysilar took it up and looped the man's arrows across his back. Another of his elves fell. These men had skill, true, but there was no way they could have cut through his perimeter without word reaching him. The answer was not important. Elves were dying. He needed a plan.

The elves that had not fallen in the opening attack were in cover and, for the moment, safe. Thysilar knew it would not last for long. The men would maneuver around and pick them off. As long as they held the trees they held the advantage. He caught the attention of the elves nearest him. "Follow me and stay together." He looped the bow over his shoulder and started climbing. Up among the leaves the battle seemed miles away. Here was another world, one Thysilar was glad to be back to. He notched one of the looted arrows to his bow and kept low. They could be anywhere up here. He gestured two fingers forward and the elves advanced.

A shadow up ahead caused him to stop. The others needed no signal. Thysilar raised his bow and sighted down the shaft. He breathed out slowly, steadying his aim, and fired. The arrow took the Falhofnan in the throat. His shot went wild as he slipped from the branch and fell out of sight. They encountered another two the same way before the humans took notice. There was not space to avoid being hit and that proved true for the Falhofnans as well, but Thysilar and his band were elves. They moved with a dancer's grace, giving the humans nothing to fire at while their own shots hit their mark again and again. Not all were fatal but the force of the impact knocked more than a few off balance. The fall would handle the rest. Thysilar ducked out of the way of an arrow, leaping forward to land on the limb of the man who loosed it. He drew his dagger before the archer had time for a proper defense, batting aside the bow and plunging the blade into the base of his neck. It slid free in a spurt of blood and he let the man's limp body drop.

The sound of steel against steel rang out from the ground below. The fighting was on in full now. Thysilar looked down through an opening in the leaves. His elves were holding against the Falhofnans who took the charge but left themselves easy targets for the archers above. Even as he watched more fell. He had to keep moving. "Pyor. Take Lyari and Triandal and continue along the edge. Nindrol and Faelyn, you two will head to other side of the column and do the same. Kill all you find. The rest stay with me and take up positions." The two groups disappeared into the dark. "Aim true." Thysilar notched another arrow, picked out a soldier about to finish off a fallen elf, and fired. The shot took him below the arm, piercing his heart. Bowstrings twanged as the others found their mark.

Thysilar lined up a fifth target when he saw Caeldeth fall. His legs twisted awkwardly beneath him, his face showing the pain his voice could not. A Falhofnan soldier removed his blade from a dying elf, smiling as he approached the wounded elf. Without word Thysilar leapt down to the waiting branches and kept going. He hit the ground with a roll and drew his sword. "Hey!" The Falhofnan turned at the shout. *That's right. Focus on me.* Thysilar leapt into a lunge that was swatted aside, bringing his sword back to block the counter swing. The Falhofnan's face turned serious, in a greater fight than he anticipated.

Their blades came together again as the human swung down trying to split Thysilar's skull. The elf turned the blade aside and quickly found himself on the defensive. Having gained the initiative the man was relentless. Thysilar blocked what he could, dodging what he could not, but still there were some that found their mark.

His arm burned from a cut below the elbow. Another managed to part the armor at his thigh. He could not last like this. He brought the next attack down, pinning the blade to the ground, and leapt back, creating the space he needed. The two faced each other down, circling. The sound of fighting had died down but Thysilar dared not take his eyes away. His sword reached for the soldier's legs but that was never its true target. The Falhofnan swung down and met only air.

His severed hand landed by his feet before he could realize his mistake. His head followed.

Thysilar allowed himself to look around then. Only elves still stood. Faelyn and Nindrol landed beside Caeldeth and helped him to his feet. Thysilar projected his voice so all the gathered elves could hear. "Take what armor and weapons you can once our wounded are seen to. Leave their dead for the wolves." He walked through the ranks with a limp, his adrenaline no longer keeping the pain at bay.

"Well fought, sir." an elf said as he passed.

Thysilar returned the nod and all the others that were directed towards him. He touched his hand to the cut on his forearm. The fingertips were dark, wet. *We deal in blood.* It did not matter if they liked him. When the fighting started they would know they could trust him.

2

What course was this? Gerold could not remember. He barely touched the soup and finished no more than half of the roasted boar. His servants were bringing out sweet lemon cakes and a collection of pies. *Good. This ordeal is almost ended.* He drank more of the ginger wine and waved for a servant to bring another pitcher. How did he ever think this dinner was a good idea?

Lady Camilla had not stopped talking since the meal began. She chewed, to be sure, but Gerold only believed that because her plates were clear when the servants came. She was well into her forties and married to the baron of Volsk, Lord Dietrich and not particularly appealing at any rate. Her daughter Letta, however, was a different matter. She had the dark hair of her father and fortunately there the comparison ended. The rest, though Camilla showed little of it now, must have come from her mother.

This was an expectation. Gerold was a baron with no wife, a detail not many others of his title shared. Nor one a Lord such as Dietrich would overlook. The opportunity for his daughter to remain in the life she had grown accustomed to was not an easy thing to ignore. It helped that Gerold was well respected by the other nobles of Falhofna. Lady Camilla seemed the type to know that the list of suitable husbands was not long. *And if she chose me it must be shorter than I thought.*

The years had not been kind to him. He was not ashamed to admit it. Where once he was busy drilling new recruits and keeping himself ready for when battle was joined, now he rarely left his study save for the occasional bath or when the situation deemed it absolutely necessary. It was no wonder the girl preferred to stare at her meal. Gerold had met her eyes maybe twice since their arrival three days ago. The dinner was long overdue.

"I'm still surprised at how large this city is." Lady Camilla said, continuing a conversation she started before the dessert arrived. "If you go by the way others talk of it you would think it was simply a military town. Not nearly so many citizens. But a castle…" Her next words were lost as she bit into a piece of cake.

"It seems the baron has been quite busy since he was given command." Lord Dietrich said. "And all while leading our armies to war. Makes me wonder why the king has not yet come out here to visit you personally."

The dagger was not well hidden. It was not meant to be. Gerold knew how the others felt about him and his coup. With his escalation of the war also came a greater need for soldiers. Soldiers that men like Dietrich had been forced to supply. "I'm sure he's much too busy to waste time up here in the cold. My letters have proven enough to keep him adequately informed." He drained another gulp of wine. "But what about yourself? I know the Lady Camilla has been hard at work breeding some of the most desirable hounds in the kingdom."

Camilla was all too eager to bite. Gerold did not listen to a word of it. Instead he placed his focus on Letta. She ate coyly, smiling at the appropriate times and looking up just enough to avoid being impolite. He was not wholly interested in her when the prospect of marriage was first brought up, but after three days with her mother's constant jabbering and her father's stream of poorly veiled insults... her appeal had grown substantially. He was sure to wear his warmest smile whenever her gaze drifted over him and kept his eyes on her as much as possible. She did not have much of a choice if he agreed but in this case he preferred the choice to be hers.

"The king himself has already asked for a pair from the first litter." Camilla finished before taking another bite of lemon cake. "This is delicious. You must give my compliments to your cook."

"Take him." The baron said.

"Oh no, I couldn't." Camilla did her best to sound sincere. Gerold knew her type and knew it well.

"I insist. It is my gift to you for honoring me with the beauty of both yourself, and your lovely daughter." He spoke to the table but only looked at Letta. At the mention of her she glanced up and met his stare. For a few long moments they remained, peering into each other. Gerold had once heard that the eyes were like windows into a person's soul. For Letta's sake he hoped that was not true. She smiled genuinely for the first time all night.

"Well in that case I accept." Camilla said with a chuckle.

"Thank you, Gerold." Dietrich said. "You are too kind a host."

I'll wager that hurt to say. Gerold thought.

"If you don't mind me asking, my lord Baron –."

"Lady Camilla, please, Gerold is fine," the baron said with a smile.

Camilla looked truly embarrassed. She had rehearsed well. "Pardon, my... Gerold. Have you given further thought to what we discussed the other day?"

Dietrich's attention was lost, drawn away from the conversation and towards a young new maidservant.

"I have, my lady, and I would rather not speak of it in front of such innocent ears," Gerold said.

"I am not a child." Letta said. They were the first words she had spoken all night.

Gerold saw a fire in her that had somehow eluded him all this time. He felt his attraction grow. *What else has she been hiding?* "My apologies, I meant no offense or implication." He nodded his head, asking for forgiveness.

Mother and daughter shared a loaded look. Camilla spoke first, the words reluctant to leave her mouth. "My daughter is right, Gerold. She will be a lady herself soon enough and should see how such things are done."

"Of course." Gerold could see the sense in it. "Speaking truthfully, your daughter's beauty is without compare. A rarity I doubt these old eyes will get to look upon again." *Don't smile yet, my lady.* "That said, there is something else you'll need to do before I accept."

Letta actually looked disappointed. Her father's attention, however, was brought back in full. "And what would that be?" Dietrich asked, making no effort to mask his suspicion.

"Volsk has been less than timely with its supplies and military aid. Both of which are invaluable in times such as these." The war was being fought by all of Falhofna, despite the other's claims about it being some personal vendetta of Gerold. *There are none of us alive who witnessed the start of this conflict. I have never known bigger fools.*

"I have sent all I can."

"And yet every other border city has outmatched you." Gerold said. "Do you mean to say their wealth is greater than yours? The king would be most interested to hear of how far the 'magnificent city of Volsk' has fallen." He had him then. It was hard enough getting through to the king being a border city. If the nobles back in the main country thought one of those cities was no longer profitable....

Dietrich was slow to respond. "I'll make the arrangements when I return. They may take a little time." The words left a bitter taste.

Gerold said nothing. He didn't have to. Dabbing at his mouth with the kerchief, he rose from his seat. "If you'll excuse me, I would like to show the Lady around her new city."

3

Not minutes after closing his eyes the nightmares returned. He blamed the wine. He should have drunk more. Letta lay naked beside him on his bed, the silk sheets contouring to the curves of her body. Not innocent at all. She left him worn out and exhausted. It should have driven him to a dreamless sleep. Lady Luck did not favor him. *When had she ever?*

Gerold slid into his robe and drank a full cup of imported southern red Dietrich brought as part of the offering. He would drown the bastard visions. They first started the night Anton returned. After seven months in the wild he looked haggard, beaten. Signs of his age had at last started to show. He told him where he looked, how far he made it up the mountain. He told him of the beasts that set upon them and the cold that claimed what they did not. Only at the end did he tell him of his failure. The baron heard nothing after that. The sound of his work, of over twenty-five years of plotting and building come crashing down around him was deafening. Anton went back to the field the next day.

The war was given whatever focus the baron had left. He removed those in command who lacked initiative and replaced them with men he chose personally. He did not have to wait long for the results. Men like Berengar would not win the respect of the nobles or have songs written about his exploits, but he would win battles. *Win enough battles...* Anton increased his number of scouts and was proving he still knew how to fight. His men had raided elven caravans and cut supply lines, taking the damned pointy-ears from the very trees they felt safest. The tides were beginning to turn.

Yet the nightmares continued.

He was in full armor but the mud had robbed it of its sheen. Its weight threatened to crush him. His breathing would become heavier, more desperate. He was struggling to rise in front of his castle. The gates were barred to him. Dozens of people – my people – stood around him, watching in silence. No matter how loudly he screamed they remained still, unmoving, watching as he died.

Gerold hoped focusing on bringing the war to its long overdue end would help keep them at bay. Every night the dreams came back. Wine worked well enough but not all the time and there was only so much in the old cellars. *Dietrich should help with that.* The city of Volsk was well known throughout the kingdom for its vast vineyards. Gerold looked back at the young girl in the bed. *She truly is beautiful.*

A sound drew his attention to the door. He put the cup down and turned the latch. The hall was empty. The sound came again, carried on a cool breeze from his study. *What was it? A fire?* Gerold did not remember lighting one. When it came again he was certain. Someone was piling wood. He took the corner wishing he had grabbed his blade. The fire was low and still young, its light shadowing the figure standing in front of it.

"Cold in here, would you say?" He was an elf. The baron could tell the moment he turned past the door. He stood at least a full head taller than him with white hair just reaching his back. A single braid was tied at the middle. He wore a nondescript brown cloak, his hands held out towards the flames. "Have a seat, please. It should warm up soon."

Gerold was too shocked to react. The elf before him showed something none of his race had until this point. He was nearly to his desk when words came to him. "You have balls, elf. Convince me why I should not have my guards remove them."

The elf mumbled something before responding. Laughter? "For the same reason I did not kill you while you slept. We intrigue each other." He turned from the fire, revealing pale skin made to look even more so by the intensity of the blue coloring his eyes and even his lips to a degree. The temperature dropped under his gaze. "Also, that young woman does not deserve to wake to such a sight." He smiled, his teeth like icicles.

"I intrigue you?" Gerold stood by his desk but did not sit. His hand disappeared beneath the polished wood. The dagger was still secure in its sheath. "You have me at a disadvantage, then. I know nothing of you."

"Yet here I am. Behind your high walls and past all your soldiers. I can't imagine the confidence in your safety being particularly high right now." Despite the subject of his words his tone held no hostility. Instead he spoke as though they were old friends, simply catching up.

"I don't know. Perspective has a way of changing things."

More laughter. Still the elf smiled. "That it does. For example, from here it is difficult to tell how close you are to drawing that blade strapped beneath your desk."

Gerold froze.

"Don't look so surprised, baron. I've been here long before you took notice. If I thought it a threat it would not still be there." He exuded a sense of surety that made Gerold anxious.

"Who are you?" the baron asked, his voice a half-whisper.

"Your mortal tongue cannot begin to pronounce my name. Truth be told it's been so long since I've heard it spoken I don't think even I would be able to get it right." The fact amused him. "Jak has worked fine enough."

The name held no significance to Gerold and he doubted Jak's true name would be any different. Whoever the elf was, it was not what mattered. "What are you?" He feared the answer almost as much as he looked forward to it.

Jak's smile somehow widened. "Now that, dear baron, is a question. One I've been asking myself for many centuries. Before I answer it there is something I would like to ask of you."

Gerold did not have much of a choice. Even if he could call for his guards the odds seemed good they would only serve to redecorate the study. And red was not one of the baron's colors. The elf was too confident to be bluffing about the power he likely commanded. Gerold was playing a new game now and had no influence over the rules. "Go ahead."

"Do you truly believe the power you seek is lost to you?" The question was asked so suddenly that Gerold was caught off guard, speechless. It was not so farfetched that Jak would know of what he sought. The power was of the elves. *But how could he know I've been searching for it?* The elf waited patiently for a response.

"If it existed I would have found it by now." They were the same words he had repeated to himself over and over like a prayer, as unconvincing now as they were then.

"I did not picture you as someone who gave up so easily."

"Easily?" Gerold felt his anger rise at the accusation. For a brief moment he considered going for the dagger once more, damn the consequences. The thought was short-lived. "You claim to know so much about me, you should know so much about me, you should know how many men I lost scouring the forest."

Jak waved his finger side to side making a *tsk*ing sound with his tongue. "It is not the trees that hold the answers."

"The mountain?" Gerold could have laughed. "I ordered men there as well. My best." *Or so I thought.*

"Three dozen men cannot adequately search the whole of the mountain in seven months." Jak approached the desk and lazily sifted through the tangled mass of maps and papers. "No matter how skilled they may be."

Gerold felt the bone-deep loss as though the wounds were still fresh. He put everything into laying his hands on the ancient power that ran within the veins of the forest. How many more Falhofnans were killed because of his prolonging of the war? To turn away would have meant that their lives were lost for nothing. All power he had would be stripped, as a start. His popularity was low enough already. *What would happen once our noble rivals to the south and east sensed our weakness? How long before it's our homes that are being invaded?* He would be lucky to avoid a hanging.

"I'm not here to remind you of your failures, though I know it seems that way. You see during those centuries I believed myself to be an outcast, forgotten by my people. Purposefully or not, I never knew." Jak's stare was distant, his smile faded. "But I had a hunch." He turned back toward the fire as a log fell. Blue flames danced in his eyes. The elf remained like that for some time.

Gerold kept silent. Like a child listening to a story, he waited.

Jak's previous demeanor returned as though shaking off a trance. "Excuse me, I was lost in my own head. This story is of no interest to you."

The elf could not have been more wrong. The baron's curiosity was peaked and hungry for any detail that helped him get a clearer picture of who he was dealing with. As Gerold saw the elf no longer planned on continuing he could no longer hold back his frustration. "You've told me nothing a determined informant could not have figured out. I've grown tired of listening." He moved to push his chair back and was confused when it refused to budge. He tried again and met the same result. Looking down he saw that the legs were frozen to the stone. His anxiety grew.

"As I said, the power you seek lies on the mountain." A cold breeze caused the fire to stir and dwindle. The window was closed. Gerold looked up to the elf. Blue eyes looked back, shining like the stars dotting the sky behind him. "I'm going to help you find it."

4

The vista came to life in his mind. Waves crashed against the rocky shore to the sound of cawing gulls. There was a light breeze, refreshing in the warm sun, carrying the scent of salt and the sea. Kris had never seen the ocean but the images here were as real as memories. He could feel the sand between his bare toes. All it would take was a push, a force of pure will, and the scene would take true shape before his eyes. Such an act was beyond anything he had done up until this point but just knowing he could do it was enough. He was not finished yet. Ships rose from the depths shedding water. Their sails billowed in the wind as the light from the sun reflected off the still-wet decks. Men scrambled to make them ready to dock. On shore were dozens of others; men and women with children awaiting the return of their family after months at sea. There would be a celebration, a feast to rival even those of the local baron. If Kris focused hard enough he could smell the boiled lobster and fried fish. When he opened his eyes it all vanished. The smells lingered for another second or two, blended together until no one was discernible from the other.

"Good." Feltahn said, his voice low and noticeably tired. "Very good. Any headache?"

"No, nothing." He had been free from the side-effect for nearly two months now, since his first real leap forward. Since then he was able to create everything Feltahn sent him. He was an artist and his muse remained perched on his shoulder. "This time was stronger, more realized than anything else."

"Yes, it would be. That was one of my more special memories. As I'm sure you've noticed, there are not very many beaches around here."

Kris laughed for the first time in a long while. The realization surprised him. *Has it really been so long?* "How long as it been? Since you were there."

Feltahn closed his eyes, visibly relaxing. "One-hundred-and-seventy-three years. It was the longest expedition that fleet had dared to go out on. They returned with enough fish to throw another dozen such feasts. There was a woman there, curly red hair, lime-green eyes that could see straight through me, to who I really was. I had been using an illusory spell at the time." He drifted away from the conversation as he returned wholly to the memory.

Kris adjusted to the cold. His senses readjusted quickly to reality, leaving him sitting on the ground as the sun was hidden behind a cluster of grey clouds. It would rain soon. "Will we try another, Master?"

The gnome blinked away his past. "What? Oh, no, Kris, you've done well enough for the day. There isn't much left for me to teach you."

Kris knew the words had to come at some point but hearing them now felt out of place. Was he really that much stronger? Nearly a year ago the things he had done now would have seemed impossible. A few days before that he would have leapt in joy at the idea of being able to leave this place and the crazy old gnome who lived here. There was not much in this Kris that the old one would recognize. He still resembled himself, of course, even with the beard. Behind his eyes and beneath his chest was another matter. But despite his progression he had still yet to use the power wielded by Feltahn against the snow giant. That, he reasoned, the gnome would get to when the time was right.

They made their way back through the slopes and rocky crags that brought them there, taking more time than Kris remembered. More than once he stopped to wait as Feltahn caught up. His breaths were labored. For reasons Kris did not know, the gnome appeared to be getting weaker since he first met him. Rarely did he go far without his staff for support and he had even lost some of his love of riddles and elaborate wordplay he once enjoyed. Kris would have let them slide as nothing more than a normal change one goes through after living with someone for so long if Feltahn had not asked for help climbing over a cluster of rocks blocking their path.

He never asked for help.

They returned to the cabin with enough daylight to set a fire by before the sun set. The view from the edge of the clearing Feltahn had built his home on was incredible. The forest went on for what appeared to be eternity, green covering a great majority of what his eyes could absorb. Upon seeing it Kris had set out to find Estelle's cabin but soon gave up. He could not even be sure what side of the mountain he was looking from. The cabin itself was small, everything inside scaled to meet the gnome's short stature.

Kris set to cleaning a deer they came across on the way back while Feltahn prepared the proper seasonings. They did so in silence, the two falling into their routine instinctually. Feltahn had an impressive wine cellar for someone so far removed from civilization but Kris stuck with his water for the night. The gnome did not.

When Kris remained seated by the fire and began poking at a weakened log with a twig Feltahn spoke up. "No practice tonight?"

Kris had used the time between their dinner and tea to continue honing his swordplay. Every night, without fail. "Not tonight. I was hoping you would tell me why you're so rundown. And without me having to pester you about it until dawn, first. It's been clear, so don't try and deny." He smiled faintly hoping to lighten the mood a bit but Feltahn was stoic, his face still and his emotions imperceptible.

When he finally did speak it was not in response to the question. "Do you remember that picture you found? Of the young woman?"

Kris was used to the gnome's ever-changing mind but still the new topic took him by surprise. "Yes." was all he said.

"I was not always like this. The mountain was once just the place where the sun always set behind. I had imagined climbing it as a child but even then I pictured this life." Feltahn was staring into the fire as he spoke, the light of the flames emphasizing his deeply set wrinkles. In truth he had not looked older to Kris than he did at that moment. "My family lived at a farm not far from the castle. The Queen still resided there, the dozens of Houses at the peak of their power. She would visit from time to time. The pigs were her favorite, though the gods alone knew why. I can still see the face her ward would make when she emerged from the pen with her perfect dress covered in mud." His eyes lit, teasing a hint of youth thought lost.

Kris felt like he was transported back to the days when he would be allowed to stay up and listen to Thysilar tell one of his adventures.

"She gave up her birthright for me. That picture was finished the day I was told that future was impossible."

"Her family told you that?" Kris asked. It would not be out of character for nobility to keep such codes, even among elves.

"No. The woman was a stranger to me until then." Feltahn responded.

"So why did you listen to her?"

Feltahn looked up at Kris for the first time all night. "The same reason you did not leave that day I brought you here. The woman, Milthrys, offered me the same power I now offer you. Like you, I was chosen to be its keeper. How could I deny such a calling?"

The answer came quickly to Kris. "You loved her. You still do, or you would have gotten rid of that painting centuries ago."

There was no response, not at first, and Kris worried that he had put Feltahn off the conversation. When he did speak Kris saw anger in the gnome's face. "I never said the decision was easy. But it was the right one." The emotion passed quick as it came. "I don't need to justify myself to you." Kris rose from his seat and went inside. He was still outside when morning came.

5

A younger Kris tried his best to hide the shiver working its way across his body. His legs ached and the feeling in his fingertips had all but gone but he was able to keep that much to himself. Thysilar could not see him shiver. It was over a year since he turned thirteen and still it had taken weeks of persistence to get him to agree. Kris wanted nothing more than to take part in all of the same things the other elves did. He was old enough now, the same age as every elf when they were allowed to join the scouts on a hunt. It was a rite of passage, the beginning of a process that would see them wearing the red and it was not fair for Estelle to keep him back for so long. All he needed was for Thysilar to feel he was a lost cause. Then what? The idea of doing his chores for the rest of his life was unthinkable. This, here among the trees and the animals of the forest, was where he wanted to be. Where he *needed* to be.

So why wasn't he enjoying himself?

The way the stories were told he should be feeling... something. Exhilaration? A sense of pride? Behind the layer of dirt there was not even a smile. It was not the soreness or restless nights trying to sleep on the hard earth. Kris had worked hard around his mother's cabin for a few years now. Even with their prey being a deer and not a Falhofnan patrol, it was not enough to put him off. He was eager but not so foolish as to think he would see real battle for some time. The cold did not bother him either, no matter what his body tried telling him. Estelle had told him that even as a baby he showed a high tolerance. Then what was it?

Thysilar looked back from his position by a moss-covered stone and Kris knew. He was not brought out here to be taught as an equal, like other elves his age were. Though he had never seen any himself he knew they had to have been treated better than this. *But they weren't human.* The two of them had travelled nearly a week in pursuit of this particular stag and hardly a word was spoken that was not an order. Gone were the stories and jokes of Kris' childhood. There was only disappointment in the elf's eyes.

"Here," Thysilar said, "It's yours." Kris hesitated, unsure of himself as nerves robbed him of his knowledge. "Now, before it runs off."

Kris hurried to his side and peered around the tree to get a better look. The stag was larger than any other he had seen before, its antlers tall and unscathed. It stood with a pride that did not come unearned. Kris drew an arrow and brought it to his bow. The string was taught, still new. He pulled it back with his full strength until the feathered haft reached his ear. The arrow wavered slightly but he kept it still under Thysilar's unwavering gaze. He could show no sign of struggle. He adjusted for distance and what little wind was present before taking one final, steadying breath. The scent of pine on the winter breeze filled his lungs. The stag cried out as it was hit, a sound it had never known before.

Thysilar placed his hand on Kris' shoulder. No words were spoken. No praise offered.

The arrow missed its mark by a little over an inch, leaving the stag dying but not dead. Its breaths were quick and short. Though it was not Kris' first kill – he had dealt with a pair of wolves that got in with the chickens. He took one with a lucky throw of a rock and wounded the other enough to scare it off. Estelle told him he was lucky they were still young. But this was different. The wolves were dealt with in self-defense.

"Take your blade. Give it a clean kill." Thysilar said.

The words brought Kris back and he did as he was told. When he withdrew his knife his hands were coated in blood, steaming in the cold air.

"When we get back you'll help clean it. Estelle will be glad for the meat." Thysilar turned to start back when he noticed Kris was not following him. "This is the way of things. He'll give us food and fur and in return be welcomed by the gods."

The words sounded rehearsed but Kris was still able to see the sense in them. He tied the stag in a bundle of cloth they had brought and wiped his hands.

Estelle welcomed them back with relief. Kris was not sure what she thought could happen to him on something so simple as a hunt but kept to himself. The overlong hug ended and he showed her the stag. She was impressed by its size. Kris had lived with her enough to see it lacked any real emotion. If Thysilar noticed the same he gave no sign. Estelle prepared her kitchen and started a fire as the others began to skin the deer, making it ready to cook. She would only need a portion, the rest put away and kept frozen to last.

The act of cleaning the meat was a bloody affair. If Kris was not comfortable with such sights before, he was now. His stomach did what it could to remain unsettled but he was able to keep himself from vomiting. He was a man grown now. He glanced towards Thysilar. The elf stood close by, knife in hand, slicing through flesh without so much as a twinge of his nose. This was what men did.

When their work was finished Thysilar turned from the pile of meat and stripped fur. "You handled yourself well."

Kris was so used to the quiet that the elf's voice took him off guard. His words even more so. "Thank you."

"For a human."

Kris took the compliment. "When will we go out again? What will it be after?"

Thysilar bore through the curtain to the question behind it. "Why are you so eager to fight your own people? To kill?"

"They're not my people!" Kris shouted back. He tugged on his rounded ears as if to emphasize his point. "They left me out to die in that storm like I was nothing."

"So it's revenge, then."

No answer.

Thysilar wiped the blood from his hands and let the rag fall. "Do you know why we wear the red?"

Kris was silent. He knew all those in the elven army wore red cloaks but never gave much thought as to why. What did it matter? He shrugged.

"Those years ago, when your... the Falhofnans came with their peace and trade, we wore browns and greens, colors more alike to the forest we call home. They refused to believe magick had truly gone." His eyes drifted to where he dropped his red cloak to keep it from getting dirty. "The red was waiting for me when I was born. It took its time getting to me, but it came. Eventually their greed came for all of my kind. For most it was when the first village burned. And the days that followed. The red came for many, then."

The elf stood perfectly still. Kris was afraid to move on the chance he would cause some sort of harm.

"It's a burden heavier than any you've felt, to carry the memory of so many souls, so much blood. So we wear the red. Their actions turned against them." His eyes focused on something unseen, his hand clenching the hilt of the knife until his knuckles turned white. "The blood they spilled will drown them." The trance ended and Thysilar's gaze returned to Kris. There was a hardness that was missing, present all throughout their trip until now. "Is that a life you want for yourself? Isn't there enough blood being spilt without you adding your own?"

6

The sun was still rising when Feltahn emerged from the cabin. With his eyes appearing heavier despite the early night Kris doubted he had gotten much sleep. He knew the feeling. His back felt twisted, knots batched together like they were plotting against him. The gnome stopped by the remains of the fire and jabbed the base of his staff through a chunk of burnt-out wood. It crumbled to ash, joining the pile. The wind would take it soon. "Come with me."

Kris was in no shape to put his mind through another meditation session. He tried as best as he could to refocus when the path they always took went by. Others were also passed, untaken. "Where are we going?"

"Up." Feltahn said, "There's something you need to see."

It did not sate Kris' curiosity to the degree he wanted but it would have to do. He learned to give up prying. Persistence may be effective with most others obstacles but not Feltahn's mind. He pulled the hood of his cloak up over his head and followed.

After a year here he thought he had experienced the worst the cold had to offer. As they continued to climb towards the peak he was shown just how wrong he was. He could handle such weather better than most, but as larger and larger flakes began to fall he wished he had brought his furs. Feltahn showed no signs of any discomfort. He hardly ever did. The way became uneven and steep. It was noon before they reached what Kris assumed to be the halfway point. He stopped with his back to a rock face, trying to catch his breath in the thinning air. Feltahn did not disagree with a rest.

"How much farther is it?" Kris asked.

The weather had settled into a state of consistency, the falling snow being added to the piles already surrounding them. Feltahn found a stone a few feet above the ground and hoisted himself on top of it. "Not much farther. Though the way will not get easier." He reached into the pocket of his robes, his hand returning with a peach.

Kris caught the tossed fruit, not realizing how hungry he was until the first bite slid down his throat. "Are you sure you can handle it?"

The gnome exhaled a long breath, not seeing the jest.

"I won't be far behind," Kris said. True to his word he was always there, never too close but ready to lend support when needed. Feltahn was struggling for a steady breath by the time they cleared the slope. He refused any assistance. This was something he had to do on the strength of his own limbs. Kris could understand that. He was not sure what to expect, having spent the long trek trying to figure it out and coming up with nothing that sounded likely. As he followed Feltahn beyond the ridge he saw that his best guesses were not even close. He stood there at the edge in a moment of disbelief.

The clearing was at least ten times that of Feltahn's. A castle had once stood here. Why, Kris could not fathom. Only its ruins remained, fragments of a picture left to the ravages of time. Pillars stood beside piles of stone where a wall once was. The remnants of a statue far from being discernible lay in what must have been the courtyard. The main keep fared best but was nowhere near inhabitable. Kris thought back to the drawings in Estelle's books. *To think something so powerful as this was brought down not by siege, but time. How can one defeat such an enemy?*

He was brought back from his thoughts as Feltahn walked toward it all. He did so casually, without Kris' awe of their surroundings and the unique charge in the air. "I felt the same when I was first brought here. Even now…. Do you know where we are?"

Kris shook his head. "No. Should I?" He tried to think of what he was taught of elven history but nothing of import came to mind.

"There are still some books that mention it. Never as a physical place." Feltahn brushed his hand against the stone as he walked by, pausing only to wave Kris forward. "Magick never left, not completely. Its effects have only become more subtle. Acting as inspiration and the like."

The prickling on his skin had a source now; one Kris had been blind to. Realization began to set in. His body acted despite his mind not telling it to. It knew.

"How many have spent the last centuries searching for the power we once knew? Even the Falhofnans have come in search of it, though they do not know it was gone long before they arrived. If only they knew the reason it left us was the very same that drove them." Feltahn chuckled, beginning to sound more like his old self than he had in weeks.

They passed under the vacant archway and into the keep. The ceiling was gone along with most of the walls, allowing Kris to see through a number of rooms and halls from a distance. Wild animals came to make the place their home, yet there was no smell such a large number should have brought. A family of raccoons nested in what looked to have been a supply closet. The sheets not too badly deteriorated were put to use. Birds of all kinds chirped from the nooks above. The two of them were given little notice. They walked over the rotted wood of the castle's dining hall and out into the back. The garden was the only thing to flourish. Weeds and wildflowers unlike any Kris had seen grew between untended bushes. As alluring as they were, it was what stood ahead that captured Kris' attention.

The pine tree towered over the tallest of the remaining structures. It was ancient, at least as old as the castle that once stood alongside it. "Older." Feltahn said. The gnome bent to pick up one of the fallen needles that carpeted the ground around the tree's base. "So much effort was spent building this mountain and myself into monsters that no one ever thought to extend their search. After all, magick would never retire to such a place." He released the needle between his thumb and forefinger, watching as it was taken on the wind.

When had that started?

Kris followed its climb, higher and higher, not once losing it amongst the thousands of others sticking from the branches. As it rose its color changed. And it was not alone. Hundreds shifted from their natural glow with reds and blues, greens and purples. None were as powerful as the first. Its light was impossible to ignore, filling his vision while the others took a second seat. He had witnessed things during his time with Feltahn that he never would have thought to see. None of it was like this. The way the energy seemed to revolve around this place, to take every stone and plant, every piece of dirt, and fill it with a sense of life. This was why the gnome had saved him, brought him here. This was why he had taken the time to prepare his mind over the last year. Kris could feel the potential that lay beneath the surface. All he needed to do was reach out and touch it.

The needle neared the topmost branch and circled it as though awaiting the right time to strike. Kris was forced to bring his arm over his eyes. It burned brighter than before, taking its place atop the tall pine.

"What I offer is power enough to defeat the Falhofnans. But it is also much more than that." Feltahn said. "Magick left our world because we took it for granted. All we can do is be patient and hope we change, prove ourselves enough to convince it to return. That is our part. It needs a conduit to live, to remain connected to the world."

Kris at last tore his gaze from the tree as Feltahn walked over to him, his eyes a deep blue.

"Are you ready to face your final test?"

7

The elf was too far to hear Thysilar's warning. Pitch burst from the flung pots and ignited, sending flames down upon Nindrol and the others with him. Their screams reached Thysilar with perfect clarity. He turned away. There would be time to mourn them later. A pair of crossbow bolts *thudded* into the felled tree Thysilar was using for cover. Bodies lay on the ground around him who were not as fortunate. He risked exposure to let loose an arrow of his own. The siege was not going well. He could not be sure how many he had lost but he knew how little they had taken. Moving along with the cover was tedious work and the Falhofnans had every area of the surrounding forest mapped out. If his forces remained where they were for much longer they would be destroyed.

But where else was there to go? The only way left between Thysilar and his elves and The Pine Fort was open ground, the trees there cleared out years ago for just such a reason. Too many had fallen already. How many more would join them without such cover for protection? And then what? Take the fort? There would still be hundreds of Falhofnans waiting behind the walls. *And the knights*.

Thysilar fired another arrow that took an archer in the chest and sent him tumbling over the wall. His quiver was getting light. They had to move.

Triandal had her troops keeping their archers busy at the west wall. Faelyn and Garavel were harassing the soldiers along the south. Thysilar remained at the northern gate. The bulk of their forces were held in reserve. He had argued with his officers over dividing their forces but in the end he saw the benefit. The Pine Fort was too well garrisoned to mount a frontal assault with their numbers. In this way the Falhofnan defenses would be forced to fracture in order to keep each attack at bay. They kept the truth of the waves' strengths hidden, ensuring the Falhofnans would not know which to devote the majority of their attention. The rest of the elves would wait with ladders ready. It all depended on whichever wall buckled first. As long as he lived long enough to give the signal.

A volley of bolts came down, claiming two more elves as the second batch of pitch exploded just behind him. Thysilar was thrown over the log from the force and heat of the blow, the back of his neck burning. He landed hard on his shoulder and cursed behind clenched teeth. *Get up, you fool.* In the open, as exposed as he was, he would be an easy target. As if in response to his fear a cluster of crossbow bolts peppered the ground beside him, one grazing his thigh and cutting through the armor. He heard shouting, both human and elven. Each vied to be heard over the other. One to save his life, another to take it away.

Crossbow strings were rewound as arrows whistled through the air. Grunts followed. The heavy *thud* of a body hitting the earth. It would not be enough.

Great chains rattled against one another, the gears squealing as, slowly, the gate was pulled open. Only a few could be seen at first, but as the passage grew the rest of the ranks came into view. Rows of armored horses stepped out from the yard, their riders in the front line with lances ready. The orange glow of the setting sun caught the steel plates, giving the knights an illusory glow, as if the fire they wielded was clinging to them.

Though a fearsome sight all their own, it was the foremost figure that inspired Thysilar's fear. Sat astride a destrier larger than the rest was The Bear. The grey-white fur of a mountain grizzly was draped across his shoulders, distinguishable from the browns belonging to the others. He wore no helm, allowing his gingered hair and beard to toss wildly in the cold breeze. There was an excitement in his face that did not belong on a battlefield. Berengar lifted the axe and howled. The echo was still heard beneath the thunder of hooves.

Thysilar rolled onto his front and struggled to stand. The archers on the wall were still firing though most of their shots sailed by overhead. The knights were gaining ground fast and would soon be in danger of their own arrows. *At least there's that going for us.* The commander was rash in committing the charge so early. Had he waited until more of Thysilar's troops were at the clearing, he likely would have broken them, ending the attack then and there. As it was he would be forced to disband his formation in favor of smaller groups which would be able to maneuver through the more forested areas. Thysilar saw the best chance he was like to get and had no choice but to take it.

The cut at his leg had gone deeper than he thought and nearly brought him back down. He was able to keep himself moving, running past his previous cover and further into the woods.

"Back! With me! Fall back!"

The elves within earshot obeyed, some remaining to fire an already notched arrow before following. Thysilar spotted the three horns he placed before the battle and took up the one he needed. The dirt at its mouthpiece stuck to his lips, mingling with the taste of brass. He blew with all the breath left in his lungs.

Dozens of hooves struck the hard-packed earth. War cries roared from the throats of the men atop the horses. The note sang out louder than them all.

Thysilar just hoped there was enough time.

Lyari handed him a fresh quiver before raising her bow, arrow notched. Forty others were lined up alongside them. More would be in position above, Thysilar knew. "Not how I'd prefer to go up against armored knights." he said.

Lyari smiled, taking her chestnut eyes off the massed cavalry to rest them on Thysilar. "None of this is how I'd prefer it to be. Life's funny that way."

He found himself returning the smile. "That it is." He let his gaze linger for another moment more. "Every minute we keep them here is time our brothers and sisters have to deal with the fort." he said, his voice raised so all could hear.

None responded. His words were understood.

"I'll watch your back." Lyari said softly.

"I'd rather you watched your own."

Berengar and his knights slowed to a trot. A few at the front tossed aside their lance in favor of a blade. The Bear scanned the forest in front of him, sniffing out his prey. For all his eagerness he was not known for being a fool. He had been campaigning against the elves for years and knew that amongst the trees, anything could happen.

Good, Thysilar thought, *he should be afraid.* The commander was responsible for scores of the elven dead. Not all were clean. The bones of his most prized victims still swung from the walls. There was a debt owed. Thysilar sought to collect it.

The elves were as still as the trees around them. They watched the knight's approach calmly, patiently, waiting for the order. Their eyesight was greater than their enemy's. Thysilar knew it would not be long until the Falhofnans made out the crimson capes between the trees. They would not have the space to muster up much of a charge, but they would close the distance easy enough. If he was lucky he would be able to fire three volleys. And with all their armor, each shot would have to hit its mark. Then the true fighting would begin.

None of us are walking away from this.

The words should have filled him with fear. The threat of death was a constant. He accepted that the moment he accepted the cloak. But never before had it felt so imminent. He expected it to feel more… final. He heard of those so petrified when faced with their own deaths that even the simplest of tasks escaped them. That was not how he felt. There was fear, yes, but not at the notion of falling. Everyone dies. It was the only true constant in this world. Instead his fear was for the elves fighting with him. His people. He did not force them to stay and fight. Most had voiced their displeasure on numerous occasions. Yet here they were, side by side, knowing full well the odds of leaving this forest.

With The Pine Fort taken, Maia and the others with her will have a clear path towards the capital and a real shot at ending this war. That, Thysilar thought, was a thing worth dying for.

"Now!"

Arrows whispered through the air. Many struck the solid portions of steel covering the knights or embedded themselves in their shields. There were a lucky few that met with less resistance. Men were knocked from their horse to be trampled underneath their comrades. Others slumped over, too entwined with the saddle to fall far. Before the elves could worry about accuracy the second volley was released. More knights fell. But not enough. The bulk split into three as they neared the elven line, the trees forcing them apart as the third volley took flight. Thysilar sighted down the arrow at Berengar. If he could cut off the head, the body may not fall, but at the least it would stumble. He took a deep breath even as the others drew their blades. Nothing else mattered. He adjusted his aim to compensate for Berengar's speed and released. The arrow raced towards its target and for a fraction of a second Thysilar thought he succeeded.

Berengar turned to swing down at an elf and took the arrow in his shoulder. The force of the blow spun him out of his saddle to collide with the ground.

Thysilar had no time to berate himself for the miss as a knight bore down on him with a mace. He ducked beneath the blow, drawing his sword as he stood back up. The knight brought his mace around for another swing. Thysilar intercepted the blow, the chain wrapping around his blade. He pulled against the horse's momentum and brought the knight to the ground. His blade slid into the soft spot under the helm and twisted, severing the knight's spine. Blood spurted as he pulled his sword free.

One.

The fighting was on in full. Elves crossed blades with knights both mounted and on foot. They were holding their own at the moment but already Thysilar could see the tide begin to turn. His elves were not armored to stand toe-to-toe with steel-clad knights.

A Red Cloak was cut from shoulder to hip, his blood painting the leaves. Another seized half a dozen openings and landed what would have been fatal blows to a less-armored foe. As it was, her attacks only scraped the beaten steel. Her head was parted from her body with a single swing. *What are they waiting for?* Thysilar rushed to the aid of a fallen elf, taking his assailant at the flank.

The Falhofnan was about to drive his sword down and end it when Thysilar struck. His blade cut into the knight's elbow, nearly severing the arm if it had not caught the elbow guard. The knight howled and turned to bring his shield around. Thysilar's sword was yanked from his grip as the flat of the shield hit him full on. Stars dotted the elf's vision. He felt his consciousness slipping. He fought against it, focusing with every ounce of his will. The knight was standing over him now, his eyes staring through the narrow slit of his helm. If his vision had not been so limited he may have seen his own death coming.

The downed elf was back on his feet. His knife bit through the mesh of chainmail between the knight's front and back steel plates. He guided the Falhofnans body away from falling on Thysilar and offered a hand up. "Sir." The elf took up the dead knight's sword and rejoined the battle.

Lyari stood amidst three fallen knights and was close to adding a fourth. Thysilar had seen her fight before, but watching at the training yard and on an actual battlefield were two entirely different beasts. And this one had much larger teeth. She was not alone. All around her men and elves fought.

Syla bled from a gash above her eye, the blood dripping down and hindering her vision. Her armor was cut in multiple places. She kept her right arm tucked close to her side, limp and useless. She fell behind a curtain of Falhofnan steel.

An elf not far off shouted something too muffled with rage to make out. He was able to cut down one knight and wound two others before he was run through.

The pair were lovers, Thysilar knew, though his name escaped him. He felt a moment's regret before returning his focus on the present. *Berengar*. He lost sight of The Bear after unhorsing him. The fighting was thickest up ahead. The elves above had fallen upon the unaware Falhofnans, pinning them between two separate forces. The Bear would be there.

A knight drove at Thysilar's torso, his blade turned aside by the elf's. Thysilar stepped in too close for the knight's longsword to be effective and rammed his elbow into his throat. He kicked out, striking his chest and sending his armored bulk into a tree where he collapsed to the ground. It would not be enough to kill him, but the wound would work in keeping him out of the fight for a while. He was not the threat.

The suffocating din of metal against metal mingled with cries of pain. Berengar's laughter stood out amongst it all. Thysilar jumped on top of a fallen log to get a better view. Berengar was covered with blood. How much of it was his own was hard to tell. He held his axe in one hand and the broken half of a spear in the other, wielding them with brutal efficiency. Half a dozen elves had already fallen. Berengar never blinked, picking out targets and attacking. It was easy to see the nickname's origin. In four swift moves the elves surrounding him were dead.

Thysilar had to act now.

A cluster of knights posed in a defensive ring around their commander. Their presence was merely for show. Berengar did not want to be spared from the battle. Any who wanted to challenge him were more than welcome to try. All Thysilar had to do was keep his eyes on The Bear. The knights did not try to stop him.

Berengar brought his axe down on a wounded elf's skull, sending up bits of bone and brain. His gaze landed on Thysilar. Without so much as a shout he was on him, leading with the spear. Thysilar was taken aback by his speed and only barely avoided a swing that would have taken him across the stomach. He brought his sword up on reflex, catching the axe just beneath the head. The attack should have been stopped there but the strength Berengar put into the swing brought Thysilar to his knees. He kept a tight grip on his sword despite the jarring force working to dislodge it. Berengar was relentless. Without wasting a minute he shifted his weight for another strike.

Thysilar dove into a roll but The Bear was too quick. The spearhead caught him at the shoulder and continued down his back, parting leather and flesh alike. Thysilar bit back his pain and returned to his feet. There could be no show of weakness. Not now. Not to *him*. He raised his sword as best as he could manage. "What are you waiting for?" he screamed.

Berengar's maddened appearance faded somewhat and he grinned. "You have guts, little elf. Until today I thought you all to be cowards." He lunged with the spear but altered his momentum at the last second, aiming his axe for Thysilar's now undefended side. The elf saw the move but too late. The axe head bit into his leg above the knee. A clean cut. "You could have stayed in the trees. The fires would have come for you eventually. But you didn't. You chose death in combat. I respect that. Now, allow me to help you." Berengar discarded the spear and brought his axe down two-handed.

And again.

And again.

Each swing was met with steel, but Thysilar could not keep the defense going. His wounds were deep and he was losing blood along with his strength. He caught a glimpse at the sky behind Berengar. Smoke was rising above the leaves. He smiled. "I think you've helped me enough for one day." Berengar turned to see what the elf was talking about when Thysilar acted. His vision swam and pain wracked his body. The strike had to be perfect.

The Bear turned in time to see the sword plunging into his own stomach, the rage too fresh for him to react properly. Thysilar pushed his sword past the armor as far as it would go before the metal caught. The wound was severe but not fatal. At least not soon enough. Berengar gritted his teeth and growled. Thysilar had nothing left. He could do nothing but watch as the man's fist rushed towards his face.

His nose broke on the first strike.

He nearly lost consciousness on the second.

The rest came in a blur. When his eyes opened again the sun was high in the sky, silhouetting Berengar and shadowing his features. "You can have the fort. It won't give you the war. The walls of the castle stand taller and thicker and will not be scaled by wooden ladders. So take it. Take your victory. There will be thousands more men soon, with fire, coming to burn this whole place to the ground. You should know that before I kill you." Berengar bent to retrieve his axe and kept it level, guaranteeing the swing would take the elf's head.

Thysilar wheezed as air entered his chest. He heard only parts of what Berengar said, the throbbing in his ears overpowering everything else. The sharpened steel was still wet with elven blood as it sliced through the air. A weight left his shoulders as the seconds slowed. They had won. *Was that howling?*

8

The Pine Fort was on the verge of falling. Kris could see that much from his position on the ridge. But it would not simply lie down and die. The Falhofnans were reorganizing. At least three dozen. And there were still archers at the far wall. It would not be enough to repel the elves entirely but they would kill many before the battle was done. *Guess I arrived just in time.* He leapt down off the edge, landing on his feet and continuing until he reached the forest floor. Following behind were the largest packs of wolves he could find. They had approached him on his journey back, likely believing him to be an easy meal. Unlike the last time he encountered their kind, this time he was not afraid. He could sense their emotions, their thoughts. Convincing them to join him was relatively simple. They were hungry. He knew where there would be food. Feltahn never told him how he knew the fort was under siege but it was not something he could ignore.

He wasn't nervous. He always thought he would be, so close to taking part in his first battle. A newly acquired confidence gave him strength he had never known. Well, a different kind of strength.

Kris wore the armor he had when Feltahn brought him up to the mountain, fixed now and reinforced with bits of steel. The plates were thinner than those found on a knight but they still added an extra layer of protection the boiled leather did not. It was his idea. The weight was nothing he could not handle, and after months of wearing it as he trained, he hardly noticed it at all. The sword at his hip, however, was new. Feltahn claimed he found it on the body of a highwayman who had wandered too close to the lair of a snow giant but Kris had doubts. The blade was still deadly sharp despite the lack of attention the gnome claimed to have paid to it, the black leather around the handle was smooth and broken in. It had seen combat. He was not sure how, but he could *feel* it. He unslung his bow from across his back and loosened a handful of arrows.

The wolves had listened to him up to now, but with the scent of death so strong, they were once again taken over by their animalistic nature, howling and rushing into the mob of steel and leather. Kris gave them specific instructions that the elves were off limits – alive or dead – and hoped that in their fervor they would not forget it. He did not have much time to worry on it. From the look of it, the fort's knights had charged out from behind the walls to engage the elves. They must not have counted on whoever was in charge having split their forces for just such a reaction. That battle was nearing its end and with the added strength of the wolves there was nowhere for the Falhofnans to go. Kris watched as one knight was brought down under a mass of muscle and fur, his screams turning to gurgles as blood filled his throat. It was the first man he had ever seen die.

He shook the thought away. Many more would fall before the day was over. His place was in the fort. Kris turned to run for the walls when a single figure caused him to stop.

Thysilar.

The arrow was in the air before another second passed. The man, who was inches away from dealing the deathblow, arched his back in pain as the point of the shaft struck him. His arms could not reach the shaft so he abandoned the idea, instead turning to locate his attacker. Kris could have ended him then and there with another arrow the man never would have seen coming. Through the heart. A quick death. But the cloak he wore was not like those of the other knights. It stood out and Kris needed a moment to remember why. He was Berengar, The Bear, the commander of The Pine Fort. Kris saw that the figures swinging from the tops of the wall above the gate were bodies and every story he ever heard regarding The Bear came rushing back.

He didn't deserve quick.

Kris let his bow and quiver fall, drawing his blade. A pair of knights moved to intercept him with steel in their hands and war cries on their lips. Kris felt the hairs on his arms rise as he reached into the well deep inside himself. He was greeted warmly, like coming home after years of being away. The magick was new to him but the two might as well have been old friends. It guided him through the routine, its energies molding as he willed them to.

The first knight's leg broke, bending backwards at the knee. His armor offered no protection. He went down screaming, all thoughts lost but for the pain.

The second had the benefit of watching his friend fall to lessen the surprise when Kris' attention turned to him. He approached with measured footsteps, his eyes open as though he were afraid to close them. His sword glowed orange, starting at the point and moving down to the pommel. He squealed, tossing it down. His fear took over. Kris extended his open hand and the sent the knight backwards with gathering speed. He smacked against the trunk of a tree and collapsed to the ground, unmoving. Now, only The Bear stood before him.

Berengar seemed to forget all about Thysilar or the fact his men were being torn apart around him. The fates of the knights did not seem to bother him. The bloodlust was on him, now. All he saw was prey.

Berengar charged headlong leading with his axe. The move was obvious, the swing too easy to predict. Instead of bringing his blade up to block he shifted his footing to where the true attack could be deflected. He had sparred with Thysilar and other elves before and knew that though he told them not to, they all held back to a certain degree. The force behind Berengar's swing was more powerful than he expected. He was put back on the balls of his feet where the attack was pressed, his blood scented in the water. Kris kept his mind clear and allowed his limbs to do the work, recalling technique from muscle memory. The magick had left him noticeably more tired, his focus eluding him momentarily. There was still much he did not know regarding his limits but now was not the time to figure them out.

They clashed again, avoiding the dead as each sought to add one more to the already high tally. A cut opened up across Kris' arm. Another nicked Berengar's ear, only missing his head by a mistimed swing. Each of the blows by The Bear left him exposed at one angle or another but he moved so quickly into the next, altering his direction within a second, that it was near impossible to seize any of them. Kris was not used to such a fighting style. There was no discernible rhyme or reason to his footwork. Every attack, whether with axe or fist, was meant to inflict the most damage as possible should it land, and nothing more. There were no set-ups, no plan to be executed like moves on a chessboard. Kris could see the sense in it.

Opponents versed in similar swordplay would know what the other was most like to do next. This way was less predictable. The next swing could come for his head as well as his legs and he would not know until their blades met. But for all his savvy in combat, there was one thing Berengar would not be expecting.

Kris pushed aside a swing that was aimed for his sword arm and countered with a lunge that was just out of reach. He stood still, watching, waiting to see if Berengar would make another move. The commander's shoulders were beginning to sag, his breathing labored. For the first time Kris noticed the blood dripping down his right leg. His weight shifted to his left. The action was subtle but not enough. *Got you.*

He opened his eyes and faked a swing left before stopping, altering it back around and to the right. Berengar would not have reacted to a straight shot. The Bear stepped down with his weaker leg and broke through the weakened layer of dirt hiding the hole Kris manipulated. He went down with a grunt, at last showing signs of the pain he was no doubt experiencing. Kris was there before he could even think about bringing his axe up, swinging down and taking Berengar's hand. This time The Bear screamed.

Blue light shined down on The Bear's face as Kris stood over him. "You're not one of them."

Kris knew what he was about to do, knew that he had to do it, but his hand refused to move.

"Nothing to say?" Berengar choked out a chuckle, spitting a glob of blood at Kris' feet. "At least if I die it's by my own damn kind. Do it."

He deserved to die. The things he did, and not just to soldiers, but the innocents as well. He was open about them, proud even. The elves were painted as savages to his people. Murderers.

He had his chance. Kris took up his sword in a two-handed grip but again he held back.

"Stupid coward!" Berengar shouted. With his final reserves of strength he revealed the dagger in his remaining hand and lunged.

Kris acted on reflex, bringing his sword down to knock the blade away before driving the point deep between the pieces of armor. He stayed that way for a while longer, listening to Berengar's breathing slow before ceasing altogether. His eyes remained open, staring out as clouds began to form. It was going to rain soon.

9

"There's still no word from the other medical camps?" Estelle took the washcloth from the elf standing beside her and dabbed at the blood around a fairly large cut. The wound was healing well, she noted. With any luck he would be back on the lines within a couple of weeks. *No,* she thought, *if he had any luck at all the blow would have taken the arm. At least then he would have been spared from returning.* "Why hasn't Maia sent anyone to check on them?"

Muriel held the bowl of warmed water as Estelle rinsed the cloth. "She has other matters that are more important. We hardly have enough soldiers to spare as it is. I'm sure the runners were simply delayed by some other errand. You know how taxing this work can be. These days especially."

Estelle knew all too well. Her house had been full to burst over the past few weeks with wounded. Space was limited so she was forced to admit only those whose injuries required the most attention, sending the others outside where she would attend them in due time. Tents had sprouted up around her cabin seemingly overnight. More every couple of days. "Yes, but they also have more help."

"I'm sorry you were dragged back into this, my lady –." Muriel started to say.

"Estelle."

"…Estelle. But everyone is needed to do their part. There's talk that Maia is coming down from the west along with Aelen and his forces in the east. Something is happening."

Estelle had heard such rumors already from a number of soldiers. She had heard them before as well. All it meant to her was that there would be more wounded to help. More bodies to bury. *And too few left to see it done.* The elf winced and she saw she was pushing down too hard. She pulled away and re-bandaged the cut. He could join the others outside. "So why are you here, then? I would think your scouts would be needed elsewhere."

"We are. I'm here to gather whoever is strong enough to join me." Muriel said, placing the bowl down on the table. "We need everyone we can get."

"There aren't many. I still have to see to at least two dozen who haven't had my attention yet."

"That will have to wait. I've already asked. Most outside have volunteered." Muriel spoke the words cautiously, like a young child admitting to breaking her mother's vase.

Estelle was slow to look at her. "I see. That's their decision." She took up the bowl and brought it over to the washbasin. "If Maia wants more blood on her hands than who am I to say no?" For a brief moment she knew the answer to that question. *Heir to the long dead throne.* Rule fell to her once her mother died, or it would have, had she not ran away. It was that very decision she found her mind wandering to a lot the past year. How many lives would have been saved with a rightful queen leading them? There would have been no infighting leading to nothing. All it decided was that there would be no Throne. The military would take command of their own regions. The war had to be won. That was the new focus. After that....

She blamed the young girl in the woods, sneaking off because he asked and she wanted. He told her it was important, but nothing else. His letters were never very long. He preferred his words to come from his own lips. She loved that about him.

"They aren't her orders, my lady. They're mine."

Estelle was too tired to mask her surprise. This was Muriel. She had lived here for nearly three decades along with Thysilar. She was ever following him around, mimicking him, and Estelle knew she had two soldiers on her hands before they ever brought it up to her. It was just who they were. She knew they had killed. She knew they had changed, as time forces you to do. She did not expect things to get like this.

"Thysilar put me in charge when he was given command of the company and we both know that's the only reason it's me standing here and not him." She stepped in front of Estelle and stopped her from walking past a second time. "I don't want to take them. But the world acts without our control."

She tried not to laugh. *That could not be more true.* "I'm not their mother. They're grown adults and can do whatever they like. If you have the time I'll at least bandage them properly before they go."

Muriel relaxed a bit. "Thank you."

Rain came down hard, softening the earth and striking the top of the tents. There were only a few amongst the group that Estelle wished had decided to stay, but their minds were made and there was nothing she said that could sway them. She told them how best to help keep the wound from festering and that, should time allow it, they should try and change their bandages every few hours or so. They nodded but she saw they truth behind the gesture. She handed

Muriel a bundle of clean cloth, folded and wrapped to keep from getting wet.

"Again, thank you. I'll try and get word to the other camps about your situation here, see if they can spare any help." Muriel stuffed the cloth in her already-full bag and looked at Estelle as though it would be the last time. She hugged her tight before turning without another word. There was more Muriel was not saying.

Estelle watched the column enter the woods and disappear behind the trees. *She wants to move on the castle.* The thought came so swiftly she needed a minute to absorb it. That would explain the added need for soldiers so soon. If Maia wanted to act so boldly – which seemed to be exactly something the elf would do – she would have had to have moved on one of the forts blocking the path. No force large enough would be able to pass without a patrol taking notice. Thysilar would have taken part. His army was the third largest and by far the closest. She turned her head towards the looming sight of the mountain, taking what little solace there was in the fact that at least Kris was still away from all this. *For now.* If Feltahn planned what she feared, knowing Kris, he would waste little time in joining up with Thysilar and the others. "He said it was important."

She did not find sleep that night. Fever had reached one of the more seriously wounded and brought nightmares along with it. He shouted and cursed, reliving a memory Estelle was glad not to be privy to. The others around were awake as well. Only Loris remained asleep. How he managed it Estelle did not know. She brought a cold towel over and wiped the sweat from his forehead. He turned and pulled at his sheets as the nightmare escalated. All she could do was wait it out.

Estelle set a fire and started a pot of tea as the wounded elf at last drifted to sleep. The water would take time to boil so she checked the dressings on the rest of the elves. One was not done tight enough while another had bled through, requiring a full change. The tea whistled before she found out Loris was dead. She would have one of the elves outside help carry him.

Her bed felt stiff and uncomfortable, her pillow flat. The rain had slowed but did not stop. It used to be soothing, its rhythmic *tap* against the roof lulling her to sleep. Not tonight. She sipped at her tea and stared, watching through the window at the way the flowers of her garden swayed along with the wind.

She did not remember falling asleep. Her eyes ached and her head was on its way to joining them. The storm had passed and the sun shone brightly, having reclaimed its place. Estelle breathed in the scent of the still-wet air, allowing it to cleanse her mind. How had she done this before? There were times when she would be helping hurt soldiers as well as raising half a dozen children. The sun would set, she would make dinner, read them a story, and still have enough energy left to check stitches. There were certainly more wounded now than she had had to deal with before but few of them required the same attention that just three of her children had. And that was spread out over years.

This was just the fifth week and she was ready to give it all up if it meant she could sleep. Was that such a bad thing? Hadn't she given back enough? *No.* Estelle cancelled out the rest of her thoughts on the subject. A fresh group of elves had arrived during the night. She would have to check for anything serious. There was an opening inside now.

"They aren't here to stay."

Estelle did not have to turn to know who it was.

"Just looking for a place to rest for a while."

"And why have you come here? I don't know if you've noticed but my hands have been full lately."

Feltahn smiled, bringing her back a century. "Aren't they always?" He looked different than before, older. Only a year had passed since the last time they talked. Not nearly enough for him to age as he had. And his eyes....

"How did you get here?" Estelle asked.

"I still have a few tricks. Though it was not as easy as it used to be, I'll admit."

Kris. So he actually did it. She was not sure how to feel. This was the second time it had taken someone from her. "Kris is...."

"He's fine." Feltahn said. "Took to it better than I thought he would."

"So why did you pick him if you had doubt?"

"I didn't pick him." He was not defensive but simply stating a fact. "Though I'm sure you'd enjoy thinking that."

"It's not the first time you would've done something to hurt me." Estelle said.

Feltahn was taken aback. She had never known him to come up short with words. "You know that's not true. If there was anything I could've done."

"You could've said no."

"It's not that simple."

Estelle was saying the words before she could think them. "It was for me." He must have forgotten. It would not have surprised her. He made every other decision without concern for how she felt about them. Why would this be any different? Kris was only a human, after all.

They stared at each other for a while. Estelle had not felt so tired.

Feltahn approached her and gently brushed his hand against hers. The skin was hard, made so from living in the mountains as long as he had. She did not mind. It was also warm. Comforting. She let her fingers spread aside to encompass his before squeezing them back lightly. "You don't have to stay here, you know. There are others who can take them in."

"And where would I go? As long as I'm here people will come. It's hard to shake over a century of reliability." Had it been so long?

"You can come live with me. I've carved out a nice enough space. I don't think your gardens will fare well but we can figure something out." The offer was genuine and it scared Estelle how much she considered it.

She gave back so much to these people, surely her debt for abandoning them was paid. As much as things had changed over the many years there was still much about Feltahn that remained. No amount of solitary living could alter that. He was still the gnome she fell in love with, was still in love with. Time may have dulled her mind of that but here, side by side, she knew it had always been true. "Don't tease me."

The old gnome smiled, "I wouldn't dare."

"I want to. You have no idea how much I want to. I'm so tired." Her eyes grew heavy, unable to blink the moisture away. "But I can't. Not yet."

"Why not?" Still his voice was low, calm.

Her thumb moved back and forth against the top of his hand, following the wrinkles that had formed there. "Them. They still need me. The other camps are –."

"Quiet, I know. I wouldn't expect to hear from them soon. It's been like this everywhere. The baron seems to be growing impatient."

Estelle wanted to ask how he always knew but decided against it. He wouldn't tell. "Did Kris…?"

Feltahn nodded. "I told him Thysilar was dug in against The Pine Fort and he went off to help. I wouldn't worry. Your boy is more than a match for any of them now."

She worried regardless. The habit of a parent. "Will you ask me again? When all this cools down."

"All you have to do is say yes. I'll come find you." He squeezed her hand back and was gone.

10

Kris scratched at the bandage around his forearm. The cut had stopped hurting and was already beginning to heal. Compliments of his new role, he assumed. The healers were not sure what to make of it. He was sure rumors were spreading about how the knights were injured the way that they were. Others had to have seen him. *Good. It will make things easier when the time comes.* Keeping his magick a secret would not do. Feltahn was wise, but in this he was the more foolish. The elves needed someone like this. Their morale was low, the enemy too numerous to make their victories feel anything but small. They needed to see that the gods had not completely abandoned them. He would be that hope, the beacon they would rally behind in the dark of night. He owed them that much.

The room around him was well-stocked with medical supplies Kris was not familiar with. Where Estelle made do with what she had, making most of her remedies from things in the forest, these appeared much more professional. Vials lined one wall with names he could not read scribbled along the parchment adhered to them. Boxes stood piled atop one another in the corner. He had watched a healer open one to retrieve cloth and other vials different from the ones already out. *With the supplies here, Estelle would be able to treat the whole of the army.* Kris pictured her trying to do just that on her own and took the thought back. He would not wish such a thing on her.

There were not many beds, most of them taken out to refurnish the larger rooms where the wounded would not be far from help. They had not figured the tally yet but Kris knew the number was high. *But not higher than the dead.* The army was all but destroyed. The few dozen or so that remained would be absorbed into the other two divisions once they arrived. Thysilar's command was over. Whether or not his victory would prove worth it was yet to be seen. The capital was an entirely different beast to overcome.

Thysilar moved in the bed beside where Kris was sitting, his eyes opening.

"Be still, my friend." Kris said, placing his arm over the elf to keep him from thrashing.

"What? Where?" His wide eyes roamed the area in a panic. "Where am I?"

"It's alright. You're at the medical building in the fort."

Thysilar was still trying to get his mind straight. "The fort? Did we take it?"

Kris nodded. "It's yours." He kept his hands on the elf's shoulders.

"Kris?" He blinked his eyes a few times as if to prove what he was seeing was real. "How did you get here?"

"There'll be time for that story another time, but I promise you'll hear it." It was an odd feeling to be on the other end. He was always the one yearning for the tales, and now it was his turn to do the telling. "How are you feeling?"

Thysilar pinched the bridge of his nose and closed his eyes tight to ward off the pain that had started. He got too excited too fast and was paying for it. "Not good. What happened? How long have I been out?"

"Four days. The healers did their best for most of your wounds. Some were more serious than others, but there were no complications. You won't be fighting for a while."

"Like hell." Thysilar said, trying to sit up. He winced, clutching his side.

"You're lucky to even be breathing." Kris said with a sterner tone. Thysilar was a soldier. He would not listen to warm words. "You won the fort, now rest." Thysilar did not argue, though Kris knew there were words he would have liked to say. *He sees I'm not who I was.* That was good. The Kris he knew was not needed right now. When the fighting was over, when it was time to rebuild... he would return then.

Outside, all the remaining elves were busy fixing what they had burned. The fires were not intentional but such things were difficult to control when in the middle of a siege. Kris was pleased to learn that only a few structures were lost beyond repair. If the Falhofnans moved to retake their fort he would prefer as much of it to remain intact as possible. They already lacked the soldiers to hold the walls and did not need to offer any other favors.

The remains of the Falhofnan dead were outside the walls, some still smoldering from the funeral pyre. Their own fallen were buried that night. Seeds were planted in the mounds. Their death would create new life. He thought he would have gotten over the smell by now, but it had yet to fade. The elves told him he would get used to it; they had warmed to him after the battle. Each had shed enough blood together to put aside the fact that their ears were dissimilar. He wiped his hands against the sides of his pants though there was nothing to clean.

"The Kringle boy?"

Kris stopped by the tents that had been added as an extension to encompass the number of wounded. An elf lay on the cot by the edge. Kris did not recognize him. "How are you?" Kris asked. It was a dumb question, but he could think of little else.

The elf raised his hand to show the missing appendages. "Can't quite put my finger on it." he said with a smile. "Don't remember me, do you? Can't say I blame you. It was a long time. You were just a boy, then. Funny how things change."

Countless elves had passed through Estelle's cabin during the years Kris lived there. The ones he remembered returned more than once, most of them being assigned to the areas nearby. How the elf still knew who he was after so many years was surprising. Especially now. "Glad to see you still have your sense of humor."

"My name's Haryk." He offered his good hand. "Thank you."

Kris accepted it. "For what?"

"I was part of the force that took the walls. We were hit hard by the Falhofnans that rallied. It's how I got this." Haryk gestured to his hand and bandaged leg. The splint poked through the bottom. "I was bleeding out, my sword buried in the chest of the man who brought me down. Then you came, a host of crimson at your back. I blacked out after, but not before seeing the fear you put in the faces of each Falhofnan who saw you." The memory caused him to grin.

Kris heard the blades clashing, men screaming. His hands felt warm as the scent of copper filled his nose. He nodded and wished the elf well before continuing on his way. Others greeted him as he passed them by on his way to the wall. He had fought alongside most of them that day and apparently made an impression.

The wall was not entirely stone. The Falhofnans started construction with that in mind but after numerous raids and setbacks they decided it would be more practical to discard the idea altogether. These bricks still remained at the base but only as a foundation. The surrounding pines were brought down and used to fortify that foundation. Over the years that followed more was added on and the wall grew. As it stood, there were nowhere near enough elves to cover it all. A pair of red cloaks kept watch on the woods below. One was leaning on his bow, the other re-fletching arrows for his quiver. Neither paid him any mind.

After the battle the wolves dispersed. Having had their fill, they returned to their homes along the mountain. Crows still lingered on the branches above the charred mass, occasionally swooping down to peck at the dead flesh. The smell was stronger here. Kris tried to get a group together to bury them but received the same answer. "No one buried *them*," they each said before pointing to the spot where elves once hung. Cutting them down was their first act once the battle was won. Kris did not bother to mention the prisoners they had taken. They were allowed to live long enough to watch their fallen burn. Then they, too, were fed to the pyre. He did not agree with it, but what choice was there? Their blood was up and revenge was all they could see. Kris could still make out the spear Berengar's head was spitted onto, at the pile's center. The flames devoured everything recognizable yet still Kris saw his eyes staring back.

Movement in the trees ahead caught Kris' attention. He spotted them before anyone else. The mass of red did not exactly keep them hidden, though they were still a good distance from the fort. It was not long before the first horn blared. Maia had brought her army. And not just hers.

Elves gathered in the square to watch as the assembled ranks passed through the gateway. *There must be hundreds*, Kris thought. *Thousands, even.* He knew that Maia and Aelen represented the last remaining strength of the elves, but seeing their numbers in one place when he had only witnessed a few dozen at most before the siege was inspiring. They could win. The Falhofnans had just as many and more behind their castle walls. *And they would require more than wooden ladders to fall. One siege at a time,* he reminded himself. They still had this one to finish. Kris stood behind a row of elves who had rushed down the stairs for a better look. He could see fine enough.

The rangers of both forces were the first to enter. They kept their hoods up, faces shadowed, with their bows looped across their backs, over their cloaks. They were the elite. What every scout aspired to be. Behind them came the commanders. Dressed akin to the soldiers they led, both incorporated more plate and chain metal alongside the leather, years of campaign and battle forever stealing whatever sheen they might have once had. Maia looked around at the parts of the wall and other structures that had been damaged, her face still. Her hair was cut short and matted to the sweat of her brow. She kept her hand on the hilt of her sword. Her eyes looked tired.

Whatever energy she appeared to lack, Aelen had absorbed. Once through the gate he walked over towards the infirmary, exchanging handshakes and unheard words with a few elves as he passed. The wounded who tried to get up out of formality were urged back down. His smile did not belong to the Aelen Kris had heard stories about. He kept his blonde hair braided at the back with his face recently shaven. He was taller than most elves, almost reaching past Kris, and lean. As the scores of Falhofnan dead could attest to, there was a fierceness behind that smile.

Thysilar was on his feet, limping out from his room. "What's he doing?" Kris asked himself aloud. He held his arm up to shield his eyes from the midday sun. Kris pushed past the mob of elves in his way and repeated the question.

More than half of the army had arrived and the square was becoming noticeably crowded. Kris hoped they had enough supplies for them all. "She'll be calling a council soon. I should be there." Thysilar said.

"I can get you when it starts. You shouldn't –."

"Don't tell me to rest. I've rested enough." He placed his arm against the tent post for support and closed his eyes. He took a breath to steady himself.

Kris knew his friend enough to leave it alone. Thysilar's mind was made. Nothing he could say would change that. *At least his command is over.* It was difficult for him to say even to himself. No matter how strongly he wanted to take action, he would have to wait for orders. And right now his orders were to remain here.

"They'll need my scouts for what's ahead."

"But your unit's been…. Are you alright?"

Thysilar was smiling. "I know these elves. I'm friends with most after serving with them for so long. They're good soldiers. But I said they'll need my scouts." He looked over Kris' shoulder as the last of the elven forces approached. Unlike the soldiers that made up the bulk of the combined armies, these elves were ragged and weary from travel. Militia. Local scouts keeping their homes safe. Kris recognized the elves from his own area. Muriel and Halfar were amongst them. They spotted him out and walked over.

"Kris? What are you doing here?" Muriel asked, staring with her mouth partly open.

He grinned, gesturing towards Thysilar. "I couldn't let him face all this on his own."

"Don't see how you could've helped much." Halfar remained a few feet back, arms folded across his chest.

"Things have changed." Kris said.

Halfar was silent.

They remained locked on one another until Kris' lips parted, the corner raising. "Stick around a while."

"This is a lot of preparation for taking the second fort." Muriel said. She had seen this dance before and did not hesitate in changing the topic. "There's been a rumor floating through the ranks. We're moving on the capital, aren't we?"

11

"Yes," Maia said, "But we cannot hope to win with a standard siege. Even if we constructed catapults." She directed the last bit towards a young captain from Aelen's force. "Our supplies are few with time foremost amongst them. The baron will be sending a force here to retake the fort. When he does, we will strike."

The walls of the chamber still held vestiges of Falhofnan flags and paintings depicting vast plains of verdant greens of their homeland. Elves had torn much of it down but still had more to go through. Maia made sure that nothing was burned until she had a chance to look through it all. With the number of books and parchment there was a chance some of it dealt with something they could use to their advantage. Information was just as valuable as blades in war. More so in peace.

"And how do you intend to do that?" Faelyn asked. In the aftermath of the battle he was promoted to fill the place of his fallen predecessor. As of yet he was unimpressive.

Aelen broke his silence. "The point of this council is to figure that out. Though I'd prefer if we had more than this damn map to go on."

Kris agreed. The first half hour or so had been spent passing the parchment around while Maia, Aelen, and their officers were caught up on the battle.

"It's not as though they go around drawing up maps detailing their structural weaknesses," the young captain said. "And since no living elf has ever made it into the city long enough to bring us any information a straight forward attack is our best option."

"With their numbers divided so, it may work," Faelyn said. More heads nodded.

Maia turned to Aelen and whispered something to him. Their short exchange ended and Maia's gaze turned solely on Kris. He knew what would follow. "You've been quiet here. What are your thoughts on all this?" All side conversations ended as a dozen pairs of eyes stared. It was not the first question he expected to be asked but he was no less prepared.

"I think it depends on the information your scouts bring back." Kris said. It was well thought by most in attendance that the baron would not let The Pine Fort be held from him for long. An army would come and it would come soon.

"And the issue of marching in blind?" El' Nir asked. He wore light robes of orange and brown, one of the few at the table not dressed in some form of armor.

A politician. Kris saw the intentions behind the question. They were dancing around what they truly desired to ask. He had no intention to play this game. "By now you've all heard the stories surrounding me. And you know I have certain... abilities." He ignored the whispers and quips. "The passages north will be watched for elves. They know how your scouts move. And going off of Thysilar's reports they know how to work around them."

"What's your point?" an elf Kris did not know asked.

"They know all of this, but the one thing they know nothing about... is me."

The assembly grew silent. Thysilar was sitting beside him, listening to it all without a word.

"I can enter the city," Kris continued, "See whatever I can about its layout and report back. I might even be able to slip into the keep. Might be there's a way to end this with less bloodshed."

"I see. And exactly how do you plan on accomplishing that?" Faelyn asked, stifling a chuckle. "With your magick?" More laughter. More jests.

Kris grinned. *Alright then.* If they would not believe words, he would give them something more. He placed the tips of his fingers to the leg of the table. The energy within him reacted to his will, funneling through the narrow path and into the wood leading to Faelyn. The elf watched, his smile fading as a branch started to grow from the ledge. Its limb reached out towards him, leaves sprouting along its length. Faelyn stretched out his hand but held it back as though the branch were some poisonous serpent rearing to strike. It bent against his pressure but did not break. The laughter ended.

"How is this possible?" Maia asked. Kris let more of the power out, allowing a violet rose to bloom from the headrest of her chair.

"Some mysteries have to stay that way." Kris said, quoting the old gnome. He returned his hand to the table's surface.

A flash of disappointed crossed her face but was quickly cast aside. There were more pressing issues at hand. "How soon can you leave?"

"Sooner would be better, I think."

Aelen was leaning forward now, his face stern. "And you're willing to take this risk?"

"I am." Kris said, "It was an elf that took me in from the cold. An elf that raised me when she had no reason. And it was elves that I watched suffer as she did all she could to mend them. There's a debt owed and I'll do whatever is necessary to see it paid."

The commanders exchanged looks too brief to be interpreted.

It was Aelen who at last broke the silence. "You'll have an escort as far as they can follow."

"No." Kris said, "I mean no disrespect. I've seen your scouts and know the level of their talent. But the road north will be watched carefully. One man traveling alone will be given less suspicion. If it looked like I was leading elves to the capital or they had any reason to believe that they would never let me live. Can you say confidently that the Baron's Falcons will not be screening everyone who tries to pass?"

The Falcons were a prominent part of the forces assaulting the forest during the early days of the war, but for reasons unknown to any here, they pulled back. Instead of launching raids they were spotted guarding a perimeter within parts of the forest between the elves and the keep.

"He's right." Maia said. All but Aelen looked to her as she spoke. "You're taking a great risk for us, Kristofer."

Kris only nodded. There would be no turning back. He wanted to help those who gave him so much. This was his chance. Now. How could he not take it?

"Are you sure about this?" Thysilar asked once they were outside. The others were still inside discussing the smaller details about what would be next regarding the fort. They were not needed.

Kris closed his eyes as he breathed in the cool air. They had not been inside for long but the temperature had noticeably dropped. The first snow would be coming soon. "Winter will be early this year." Muriel and Halfar had seen them leave and made their way over. "When I was up in the mountains I read a story about an elf,

146

one of the first to settle this far north. He was young, eager to leave home and set out on his own, start his own life. He had some experience with woodcutting and construction having grown up on a cattle farm in the southern territories and felt confident he could build himself a nice enough home. But he knew nothing about the winters.

"His crops died, along with his livestock. Illness gripped him, the cold creeping into his bones. No matter how large of a fire he tried to build it was not enough. Then one morning he woke to find the snow had stopped falling. In place of the white the ground was again brown and green, life returning. He survived. Frost took three fingers from his hand and nearly left him without a leg, but it did not kill him."

When more than a minute passed in silence Halfar spoke. "I heard something similar from my mother near every night before my older brother started teaching me to use a sword. But the story featured a squirrel and a stash of acorns instead."

"Estelle told the same." Thysilar said, "But that was about greed. What does this have to do with anything?"

Kris blinked as though returning from a daydream. "You can't know you're ready until you try."

"And if you fail?" Thysilar asked.

"Then I guess we'll know."

12

It was an odd feeling, having to rely on a fire to warm his bones. *When had it gotten so cold?* Feltahn rubbed his hands together by the growing flames but it was pointless. The joints remained stiff. He decided to make himself some tea. Each day he felt things change, his mind amongst them. He was not as quick as he used to be, even taking more time to grasp what he was reading than it used to. That he did not expect. The magick had prolonged his life far past the point when it should have expired. He knew better than to think once it was gone that he would simply pick back up where his life had been left, but did not think the transition would come so swiftly. *Maybe it'll slow once it reaches a balance.* He doubted it but clung to the thought regardless. It was barely over a week since he spoke to Estelle, and he planned to make good on his word.

His fingers fumbled with the tea leaves but after a few minutes he managed to get them settled. It was a little sweet having knocked the sugar over and into the cup but he preferred not to make another kettle. Feltahn only brewed enough for himself. The fire had at last reached a decent size and he sat at his chair in front of it. Combined with the warmth of his tea he finally began to feel a measure of comfort.

The flames dwindled under a sudden wind. It brushed Feltahn's skin, sending a harsh chill throughout his body. He groaned as he lowered himself to his feet. All the windows were closed and had not been open in decades. Hot summer days were not a worry up here. The door was similarly locked. *Then where...* He opened the door to his bedroom. The sound of old metal squeaking against itself did not disturb the elf sitting at the edge of his bed. His profile made it impossible for him to be Falhofnan. No relief was felt from that knowledge. The air beyond the door was considerably colder. "What are you doing here?"

"I'll admit I'm surprised to find you living here." The elf's breath frosted in the air. He had a picture frame in his hand. The drawer to Feltahn's nightstand was open. "The mountain made sense, I can understand why you chose it. But this," He looked up and around at the rest of the room. "With the power you have I would have thought you'd build a castle here."

"This fits me fine enough."

The elf chuckled. "Yes, I suppose it does, doesn't it? A bit lonely though, I imagine." He looked down to the portrait in his hands. "Too cold for her?"

Feltahn was without his magick but not his intuition. He still remembered what that power felt like, how being in the presence of it set your hairs on end. It radiated off the elf in waves. "Is there anything I can help you with? If you're seeking shelter for the night...."

"No, thank you. The cold's never bothered me." He put the picture down on the bed and stood. "As to your first question, I think it's best discussed over a drink. After you." The elf waited for Feltahn to step back from the doorway before walking out into the firelight. He was tall, with his pale skin and blue eyes ensuring the gnome would never again confuse him for another. Despite his youthful appearance Feltahn could sense the age that lay beneath.

Who are you?

The elf opened the cabinet by the icebox and took down a bottle of vodka Feltahn had not touched in years. He grabbed a pair of glasses and motioned for Feltahn to take a seat. "My name is Jak. I apologize for arriving the way that I did. I know how it must look." He poured the alcohol into both glasses and handed one to Feltahn, taking a generous sip. "Where did you get this?"

"I'm not sure." Feltahn said truthfully. He had travelled much in his life and found it difficult to recall the dozens of places he had been. His sip was small and burned on the way down. The second was not as bad.

"The years do take their toll. I know you wouldn't think it by looking at me but I've lived for nearly as long as you, give or take a few decades." He finished his glass and poured another, filling it half as much as the first. "But enough of all that. I can see you are a busy little gnome and this is not how you intended to spend your night so I will cut right to it. The power you have was never meant to be yours. I was young when it came time for my mother to pass it on. Too young to entrust such power to, or so she told my father. He was an angry man on the best of days, and quick to temper. But his intentions were always pure."

Feltahn kept his eyes on Jak, occasionally bringing the glass up to his lips. His mind may have been slower but there were moments in his life he would not easily forget. The day Eldrith came to him was one of them. She had nothing with her save the clothes she wore and the few items in her bag. Books mostly. Feltahn had been too focused on her words to think on anything else. The clues were there, beneath the projection of strength. She was leaving something behind in the same way he was. *Only she no longer had this responsibility to keep her from returning to face it. Or its strength.*

The power Jak hoped to attain here tonight would not be his first taste. And Feltahn was sure he did not learn it himself. "Your father had some power also." he said, not waiting for Jak to pause before speaking.

The elf took no offense. "The people of my father's village had gifts, he told me. Before the great fire could destroy them all he was able to save a few things. He taught me what he knew, yes. Promised me I would be able to restore those ways. It was my birthright." The fire dwindled and the room darkened. "And she took it from me."

Feltahn fought back a shiver. "I knew that village. The kind of sorcery they practiced –."

"It was not sorcery!" Jak said, "It was true power." Wind buffeted the walls and windows outside as the snow fell harder. "We were the ones left unharmed when magick left the rest of you behind. It was my people who were meant to rise up, to lead our race out from the dark. My mother was the first sign. Magick went to her so it could be given to me, to take my rightful place at the head of change."

Feltahn had a good deal of time on his hands during his long life and spent much of it reading -- fiction, poetry, but nothing as much as history. He wanted to know more about what it was he was keeping inside him. Magick had left the world long before his time, or so he thought. During this research he learned of Nox Aeterna and the people who lived there. *But that sect was destroyed nearly a millennia ago. No matter how powerful his father was, he could not possibly have lived so long to father a son.* Feltahn wanted to believe that. He wanted this elf to be nothing more than a trickster who had picked up a few things on his travels. But his eyes, the cold that seethed from his very being.... That sorcery had survived the purge and found a new host. *And it would die with him.*

The gnome thought it cruel to come against the most dangerous enemy he had had to face a mere week after giving up his power but knew he could not allow Jak to leave. "Do you mind if I add another log?" He emptied his glass.

Jak appeared lost in his own mind and was slow to respond. "What?" he asked, snapping the question before controlling himself. "Yes, by all means." His smile came too quickly.

A pile of wood was stacked by the fire. It had grown smaller since Kris left and Feltahn had to go back to cutting them himself. He leaned his cane against the brick bordering the fireplace and picked one up. With his other hand he took an iron stoker from the rack. He shifted the burnt out logs to reveal the bright orange beneath. The thin wood caught quickly enough. He lingered longer than he felt he should have. He had never been the best when it came to fighting even when he had magick on his side. *Just do it right. All I'll need is one good hit.*

Feltahn took the wood in his hands and brought it up level with his face. The fire at the end blurred Jak's image on the other end but he was there. The vodka in his mouth came out in a spray. It touched the flame and ignited, projecting the fire towards Jak. The elf shouted his surprise and pushed the chair back to fall on the floor. Feltahn wasted no time. He had the initiative and could not let it slip. His grip on the makeshift club tightened as he ran forward and swung for Jak's head. Instead of the softer impact of wood against flesh the log clacked against the wood of the floor, jarring his arms and threatening to weaken his grip. But he held, lifting the log up for a second swing.

A strong wind pushed Feltahn back into the side of his armchair. All light went out save for what little the moon offered. He kept his club in front of him. His arms trembled, his breathing quick. It was cold in the dark.

Movement to his left caused him to act, swinging wildly and with every ounce of remaining strength left to him. He met only air. Icy hands gripped his neck and forearm, stealing the air from his lungs. The log fell to the floor. Cool blue eyes appeared, cold and staring. A thin layer of steam rose from Jak's face.

"That was not very polite," he said through gritted teeth. His voice was shaking, calmness and anger fighting for control. He twisted Feltahn's wrist, snapping the bone. The gnome had never felt such pain. "I'll ask once to give me…." His words trailed off and he stepped back, taking the gnome still suspended in his hands. He squinted his eyes and turned his head away before returning to look at Feltahn again. "What did you do with it?"

Feltahn's words refused to form, gasps coming in their place. Jak took the hint and released his throat, still holding him up by his broken wrist. The pain was threatening to overwhelm him but he pushed through it and smiled. Feltahn kept his eyes open, unwilling to flinch.

Jak's eyes closed and his head sagged. A single deep breath exhaled through his nose. Feltahn almost didn't notice the blade slide between his ribs. All he felt was the cold, empty and all-consuming.

Winter's tendrils spread from the wound. Feltahn could feel his body begin to fail. They were reaching for his heart. *He's stronger than I ever was. He'll succeed where I couldn't.* Jak would come for him too, Feltahn knew. The 'how' of it was less certain. Other questions and images passed by, from the first time Estelle brought him to the palace, to his visits south, where the deserts ranged like vast oceans.

They faded, one by one, until only a single image remained. For a moment he stood in the sun, a warm breeze caressing his skin. She always loved the gardens. Would have one of her own, she told him. Larger even than the one surrounding the palace. He smiled when he heard it. *She didn't say no.* When he opened his eyes it was not to Jak's face, but Estelle. Her dress caught the wind as she smiled, offering her hand. The centuries melted and he was with her in the glade. They shared their first kiss beneath these trees. His fingers brushed against hers. They were softer than he remembered.

III

1

The night sky was clear. Rank upon rank of stars shone in their thousands. The moon was slim but no less present, looking to Gerold like a general amongst his legions. He longed for the days when his time was spent addressing battle plans, moving from fire to fire, getting to know the men who had placed their lives in his care. His eyes ached and he rubbed them with the palms of his hands before taking another drink of wine. The bottle was getting low. He would have to go down to the cellar for another case. He stared at the unrolled parchment in his hand a moment more before tossing it into the fire. The words were the same as the dozen others he had received, more or less. It was the inherent urgency that changed.

Gerold had watched the king's seal burn over a dozen times and then just returned to his desk. His headache continued unabated no matter how many glasses of wine he drank. Not even in the arms of his new young bride did he find solace. His clothes practically wore him, he had grown so thin. He no longer recognized the face that looked back at him in the mirror. *Has it truly been only a year?*

The question was one the baron asked himself many times in recent weeks. Time had seemed to drag on, extending the hours of each day until he was surprised to find the sun rising. *He promised to deliver their power to me, yet all he's done is make demands.*

Since Jak first came to him that night in his study Gerold was faced with increased pressure from the capitol. The king wanted updates on the war, a timetable leading towards its end. *If I knew that the war would already be finished.* He knew the true pressure was from the other barons but it was not them making the demands. Because it was the king's name at the bottom of the letters, each one he let burn without a response was tallied. It was only a matter of time before someone was sent for answers. He needed to have the magick by then. If not…. The thought of his body swinging in the courtyard was not one Gerold enjoyed. *And with The Pine Fort falling to the elves, I have no choice but to send more troops to retake it.* To do otherwise would only spur his opposition even further. Why should he be allowed to lead when he cannot even hold on to his own lands?

Atop the pile of documents clamoring for his attention was the list of troop numbers he had requested. He read them over dozens of times, each time hoping they would change, that he was reading them wrong. *The elves could not have picked a worse time to grow a backbone.* The last twenty years had been quiet, albeit unproductive, and it seemed to be the moment of calm before the headsman's axe came down. Gerold could almost feel the metal against his neck. He needed every sword here, manning the walls and aiding with the fortifications. Only time kept the truth from the other barons. Only time between his castle and their armies.

And the king would allow it. Without his barons he had nothing and he knew that. It was part of what made him such an effective ruler. He kept them happy and they kept his kingdom running, supplied it with manpower to keep it secure. They all had their purpose. All except Gerold. The only thing he had contributed was debt and orphans. That would be his legacy. The historians would not bother to dig beneath the surface. History had no time for myths and elven bedtime stories. It would be easier to label him a tyrant.

The papers crumpled under his hands. He reached for the bottle of wine and tossed it against the wall, the shards of glass scattering across the floor.

"My lord?" Anton stood at the door with his hands briefly by the daggers at his side. A year on the front had left his armor worn down. There were more line on his face than Gerold remembered. He forced Anton from his side after failing to locate the source of the elven magick and his Falcon's had been busy ever since. It had been over a decade since Anton was in the field but he appeared to have lost none of his edge.

"Anton," Gerold asked, taking deep breaths to compose himself. "What are you doing here?"

The scout's demeanor was unchanged. "You sent for me." His hands relaxed away from his blades.

Had I? The baron did not remember even hearing his old friend had returned. Perhaps the wine was stronger than he thought. "Yes, right. What news do you bring?" It would be easier to go along. He did not need his moment's forgetfulness to grow into rumor.

Anton took slow steps into the study, each one betraying his uncertainty. "We've been harassing the elven forces in the area, hunting their scouts and raiding what supplies we can find." He looked down at the glass and stepped around it. "I thought to take their main force head on. The commander was new but seemed determined to make some sort of name for himself. A busy bee, that one."

"And you failed there as well." Gerold said under his breath.

Anton heard. "I underestimated him. This was all in my report."

Gerold stared into the fire. "Why are you here?"

"Because you sent –."

"No, why are you here in the city? Why did you return?" The letter was almost completely ash now.

Anton was cautious with his answer. "We were out there for over a year without leave. After the battle I thought it would be best for the men to catch their breath, see their families."

"And disobey my orders." Gerold turned away from the dancing firelight. Anton's eyes remained as fierce as they had ever been and he met them without falter. He was still unsure why or when he sent for him but an idea came to mind that made him glad he did. "How many do you have?"

The answer took a moment but Anton gave it with surety. "Two hundred and seventeen."

"And they're all able to fight?"

Anton nodded.

"Good," the baron said. He looked back down to the mass of papers on his desk and sorted through them. He knew it was there. Yes. The city looked small on the map. He scanned the rest of the notes he had written to make sure he was not mistaken. "Yes, that should work."

Anton remained silent.

"Yes," Gerold said again as he repeated the plan in his head. "I suppose it's good that you're here. With The Pine fallen I'm sending Dmitri with most of the Third to take it back. The walls will be undermanned without them. You'll divide your men and attach them to the soldiers already stationed. If they're as well trained as you claim them to be they should make up for some of the loss, at least." He let his words hang in the air. Anton was not meant for such a stagnant position. He had said so himself numerous times. He needed to be moving, always from target to target. *He made his own fate.*

"As you say, my lord." The words were forced. Gerold knew that. But whatever resentment Anton was feeling would be put aside. Dangerous an enemy as he was, he held his loyalty above all else. He would man the walls for as long as was necessary.

Gerold could see the dozen banners in his mind, moving in the wind as they climbed over the hills ahead of thousands. *Anton's men would only slow them down. But time was worth more than the lives of his men.* Given enough of it Jak would return with the power he promised. Then it would not matter how many men the barons assembled. All would see his true measure then.

"If there's nothing else, I have work that requires my attention."

Gerold waved him off without a word. The Lady Letta was asleep when he finally returned to his chamber. For a moment he was tempted to stay there, leave her to her dreams. The bed was large even when they were in it together and her body seemed to be swallowed by it now. He felt his balance wavering. How many bottles had he drank? The cool breeze from the open window threatened to blow him over. Gerold slid from his robes and climbed beneath the collection of pelts draped over the mattress and the young woman sprawled on top of it. She stirred at his touch but it was not the comfort of her body that he sought. Gerold moved his arm behind her head, his other hand resting on the small of her back as he pulled her in close. Letta's lips came down on his wrist, kissing him softly until reaching his hand. She felt warm. Not like that of a fire or the furs wrapped around him. Truly warm. She reminded him of home.

2

What surprised Kris most was the smell. He had grown up in the forest a few days travel from the nearest settlement and fresh air was not something he found himself wanting of. Walking the muddy roads of the lower quarter, with rundown shacks on either side and empty eyes following his every step, he wanted nothing else. The people here were packed on top of each other without regard to comfort or cleanliness. More than once Kris had walked past emptied waste pails and piles where, to his best judgment, they simply squatted there on the road. It was clear to him that whatever good intentions the first baron may have had fell short with the growing population. Whether the war was to blame or the lack of a proper plan, Kris was unsure. Regardless of the motivations, the city was divided. The poor lived in the area bordering the inner walls of the keep while the even less fortunate found their way here. *How can they live like this? They feel safe behind these walls but they're treated no better than beasts in a slightly larger cage.*

He passed a child playing with a collection of rocks. The girl could not have been older than five or six. Dirt caked patches of her hands and some spots at her face. Her blonde hair was muted and un-cleaned, hanging down by her face. She never looked up at him. Not once. And she was no elf.

Out of everything he saw since passing through the gate, that simple realization was the most difficult for Kris to grasp. The only men he had seen that were not in Estelle's books were either dead or trying to kill him. Here, however, he was just another loner walking the streets with his own reasons. They would look his way but with nothing more than a casual curiosity, perhaps wondering if they had seen him before. What reason did they have to mistrust him?

While the First and Lower quarters had obvious differences, there was one unifying factor that Kris noticed. In the forest there was always color. Browns, oranges, and reds in the fall. Blues and purples in the winter. Each town and village was vibrant, using the wildlife around them in their own ways. Here everything appeared to be viewed through a haze. Whatever it was that clouded the air he breathed clung to the surface of everything within the wall, to one extent or another. The only colors here were cold. He had seen enough to know what needed to be done. If the Baron could do this to his own people, how could he be expected to honor any words of peace they might have offered? Gerold would settle for nothing but their complete destruction. That reassuring fact was enough. Kris could not hold back. And he wouldn't.

Kris had played the role of a trader whose wares were abandoned during a frontier run. Elves had cut down his fellows, leaving him lucky to have survived. One of their band was efficient with his war hammer and drew enough eyes to allow his escape. The story was important. He was unsure how trusting whoever he came upon was going to be. It would have to be enough to convince anyone from another trader to one of the Falhofnans' Falcons. Fortunately it was the former.

They did not talk about much, but when Fynn learned Kris was from one of the villages outside the city and had never actually visited the city before, he kept going on about the pub. There were more than one, Kris found, but still Fynn referred to this as though it were the only one that mattered. When Kris asked where it was the trader laughed. "You'll know the one." The old man's confidence was well placed. Kris had not even started to look when he found it.

The pub was placed on the road between the lower quarter and the rest of the city. As far as business sense went it was a smart move. No sign hung from the wood to state its name. Instead a handful of worn stockings were nailed to the overhang of the roof. A dozen men stood outside the door and along the wall, each in varying degrees of drunkenness. Some with bottles still in hand. Kris could smell them from where he stood. He did his best to keep the displeasure from his face as he walked by them. Aside from the few comments a small group directed his way he pushed through the door without incident. The scent that greeted him was stronger than he was ready for. Tobacco smoke filled the air and Kris was sure it masked the worst of it. For that he was grateful.

A quick count told Kris that over forty people were sitting at the bar or the tables around it, another dozen standing. Men joked and laughed between drinks, getting louder after each. Women walked between tables with trays balanced on their hands. Kris watched as one of the rowdier groups grew more forward with their server. She smiled politely at their words but otherwise tried to ignore them. It was when they started pulling at her dress, her arm, that her politeness vanished. "I told you before to keep to yourself, Harold."

Harold's expression and half-open eyes told Kris that he was drunk. "My boys here have had a long week and I told 'em they'd have themselves a good time tonight." He reached his hand out again and squeezed the base of her back. She twisted away from his grip but that only made him angry. Harold stood, pushing his chair to the ground as he all but lunged for the girl. She shouted as the tray fell, the empty glasses breaking against the floor. Harold took her arms in his hands and pinned them to her sides. "You can't expect me to look like a liar to my boys."

The man behind the bar passed a wary glance in between shuffling glasses. A few others looked up from their food and drink but otherwise made no motion to help. The laughing continued almost completely unhindered.

There were five of them including Harold. Too many for most to think of taking on. Three of them looked accustomed to a fight.

The woman continued to struggle, slamming her forehead into Harold's nose. It bled, leaving a smear on her light skin. That he did not appreciate. He risked letting one of her arms go to raise his fist. It came down fast but never landed. As fast as the blow was, Kris moved faster. He caught Harold at the wrist and clenched. "Let her go."

Harold's friends stood, all joviality drained from their faces.

Kris kept his composure calm. He did not want a fight. "I'm sure whatever it is you're looking for you can find someplace else. I think I saw a few just down the road."

"You best let go of my hand, boy." Harold tried to pull free but could not budge.

Kris said nothing and just stared. He caught the man's unfocussed gaze. Harold's face grew slack and Kris nearly reeled back from the waves of images that came flooding into his mind. They were memories, but not his own. They belonged to Harold. Kris saw moments as far back as his youthful years, playing with the local kids up until things that could not have been longer than a few weeks before now. Some were pleasant, filled with genuine joy. Others were not so joyful. And they were piling up. As they began to fade Kris saw that he was not the only one to experience the visions.

Harold saw them as well.

The strength in his arm vanished and his lips parted. "How did…" Any words past those failed him. The men behind him stared on in confusion, wary to act with Harold's sudden shift. None dared to look at Kris.

"Leave." Kris said, letting go of Harold's arm.

He waved his fellows over and left. His eyes never drifted higher than waist level.

"Looks like he left extra for you." Kris said, revealing Harold's coin purse. He took the coins and shuffled them between his palm and fingertips. The girl stared at him but made no other move. Most of the bar had also turned their attention his way. *What was that?* He placed the money in her hand and closed her fingertips over the metal.

A stool opened at the bar and he sat. Only then did he realize he had no idea what to order. Maia made sure he had coin enough to make it a week if necessary and he took the purse out. "I wouldn't let too many people see that." the woman beside him said.

"Sorry?" Kris asked.

"All that silver will draw attention you don't want." She turned away from her golden brown pint and looked into his eyes. "They aren't glowing anymore."

Kris took a single piece of silver out and quickly returned the others to the pouch by his hip. He caught the bartender's attention and hoped his anxiety did not show. Feltahn's eyes did the same during his stay in the mountains but Kris never gave it much thought. The more he did now, however, the more the old gnome's tricks made sense. What Kris saw came directly from Harold's own mind. *The same way Feltahn seemed to know what I was thinking.* It was like a muscle, this power. And like every other muscle he could build it up, learn to use it, control it.

"Maybe I have to get you angry, like Harold before he ran out with his tail between his legs." The woman finished her drink and was brought over another without having to say a word. "Though it doesn't take much to scare that dog. Meaghan over there is new, but she'll learn. He tried that on me once a few years back." She smiled, hiding the grin behind a fresh glass.

The barman stopped in front of Kris and asked what he wanted. Kris looked around at the mugs the others at the bar were drinking. Dark, light, the scent of honey wafting from one with a heavier, more hoppy aroma clinging to the others. Each alluring in their own way but none of it helped with his problem. How could he order something if he didn't know what to call it? It was possible he could play it off as being unfamiliar with such brews in his village but suspicions were already raised from his entrance.

"He'll have a Patch." the woman said, sliding a few coins over. "You'll like it. They use rum barrels to hold the ale."

Kris nodded. "Thank you." He turned to her and got his first real look. She had red hair down to her shoulders, pulled back and away from her face. Freckles dotted her skin in places, more so beneath her eyes.

"It's not polite to stare. Or to let a lady buy you a drink without giving your name."

"Kris." he said. The barman placed the drink down on the bar and Kris brought it to his lips. The cool liquid was smooth as it passed down his throat. He was unused to the taste but kept his reaction from his face. It wasn't bad.

"Hello Kris. Katerina." She offered her hand and gave Kris' a light squeeze. Green eyes locked with blue. "How do you like it?"

Kris took another sip, breaking the stare. "It's good." he said, unable to think of another way to phrase it.

"Takes some getting used to. Haven't been to the city much, have you?" Katerina asked.

Kris shook his head. "I was raised on a farm outside of Nestor."

"Haven't heard of it." Katerina said. She turned on her stool so she was facing Kris, her arm resting on the bar.

Kris did the same. "I'm not surprised. It's a small village to the south. We don't get many travelers."

Katerina's eyes shifted at that. "The south, huh? Didn't mark you as the type."

"What type would that be?"

"The type that would work a farm so close to the elven border."

The drink bought him time to think. He had to be careful here. "Heard stories, have you?"

Katerina shrugged. "No different than any other you must've heard. Can't say I believe they're as savage, but they don't have much reason to like us.

No they don't. "I don't imagine there are many others that share those feelings here."

Her smile brought out his own. "Here, no. But you'd be surprised the things you'll hear in the square. We're not all like you country boys think we are." She flashed Kris a look and smirked above the rim of her glass.

Kris smiled back. He was beginning to realize that. "So what do –." His words were cut off as a large man with an overhanging gut pushed his way in between the two of them, his arms around both of their shoulders.

"All night I've been here and not one drink did I buy you." His breath stank, causing Kris to turn away. Katerina showed no signs of discomfort. "George! Another round for the Goddess and her young friend." He turned his attention on Kris, regardless of how much Kris wished he hadn't. The man slurred through his words before becoming understandable once more. "You have to be careful with this one, boy."

"I'm not a boy." Kris said with as much politeness as he could manage.

The man laughed with his whole body. He reached up and patted Kris' cheek. "Take's more than a few whiskers." he said with a wink. He dropped more coins than were needed and returned to his table.

"Sorry about that. Markus was never good with manners." Katerina said.

Kris finished what was left of his drink as his anger subsided. "It's fine. The Goddess?"

"Outdrink the biggest men in the city and word spreads around the pubs. As names go, Ale Goddess isn't one to complain much over." She swallowed the last gulp and pointed to Kris' empty glass. "Another? I think Markus left enough for two."

The alcohol was already present in his mind and Kris could feel his body trying to force it out. For a few moments he wanted nothing else but to order another. Katerina watched him, her eyes stirring his blood in a way he had not felt before. His thoughts were caught up in the shroud of white noise the tavern produced. It would be easy to stay. "I have to go."

"So soon?" Her body leaned closer to match the altered tone of her voice. Kris noticed the holly leaf pendant around her neck as it caught the light of the nearby fires. She smelled like pine. "Not much a farmer has to do in the city. Not once the sun sets."

"There is tonight." Kris turned to leave when Katerina stopped him, her hand grabbing his arm.

"If you find yourself here again tomorrow night, stop by the library. I'll be there for a few hours."

The notion took Kris by surprise. While he tried his best not to his face must have betrayed his thoughts.

"What? Just because I spend my nights here with people like Markus I can't appreciate a good book?"

"I didn't –."

"Too late. I'd say you owe me at least three drinks to make up for a remark like that." Her serious demeanor dissipated some. "But you'd be surprised how many of my students' parents think the same thing."

"A teacher." Kris said, his tongue moving faster than his mind.

"Careful. You're cute but it'll only get you so far."

Kris had enough sense not to respond this time. Katerina gave him a last smile and returned to her seat at the bar. Again he felt the temptation to join her. It would almost be easy. The drink was warm as was her company. Together they helped keep away the screams. He could already feel their weight returning. But there was still a war to fight. His friends, people he cared for, were still fighting it. That was why he came here.

The air seemed cooler as Kris stepped outside. The men by the door were still there but had turned their dwindling focus to a patrol passing by. He ignored them. In the distance, maybe a quarter of a mile, he could make the tip of a castle tower. The baron would be there. *It could all end tonight.* Kris thought of the library by the main square. He had noticed it earlier on his first walkthrough. It would be there once this was over.

3

The area surrounding the inner wall was sparsely guarded, considering the importance of those behind it. That was not to say it would be taken easily. Soldiers paced the narrow walkway in ones and twos, not leaving enough space for Kris to feel overly comfortable. He was getting ahead of himself. What he would do once atop the wall did not matter if he could not get there first. And that was proving difficult. Kris thought about trying to scale it by hand but that idea did not last long. Even the most secluded area would leave him exposed once he cleared the cover of the nearby rooftops. He considered jumping the distance from one of the higher buildings but faced a similar issue. In the time it would take for him to both find the right place and read the guards' movements to time it perfectly he would be spotted. The chance was too great. For the first time in over a year he felt as useless as Halfar kept reminding him he was. He and Muriel were the scouts. They had the experience. He was just a young man fresh from Estelle's cabin with no idea how the world worked. Even now, with the power he had, he still needed time to fully understand it. *If I hadn't rushed off like a damn child.* He lashed out, punching through the window of the house behind him. Blood dripped down the tips of his fingers. The frustration diminished but not by much.

This was not going to help. He needed a clear head. His mind worked through techniques Feltahn had taught him. Air was breathed in and out at slower and slower intervals. Kris opened his eyes. The magick had spoken to him before. Once during the battle, and few times again as the elves worked to clear away the debris left from the siege. Kris controlled it then, albeit with help. If he could get past that first seal he knew he could do so on his own.

The city grew quiet as the night carried on. Darkness spread in the dim moonlight. For an hour Kris sat in an alley with his back against a wall, scouring every part of his subconscious. It had to know he was searching. What he heard outside the fort was a voice. Barely a whisper, but it was there. The magick was very much alive and refused to make things any easier. He had to prove himself. Show that Feltahn made the right choice.

His fingers fit into the cracks between the stone and allowed him a decent footing as he started to climb. The house he chose was not the tallest but that was the point. Here he was at his most vulnerable. The less time spent there, the better. He reached for the ledge of the roof and hoisted himself up onto it, rolling over to his stomach. His eyes locked on the wall ahead and the men moving above him. They continued as usual. He had not been noticed. *So far, so good.* He waited for the pair to pass and rose to a crouch.

Across the gap the next building stood a few yards taller. Kris took a single breath before he rushed forward and leapt. The sole of his foot brushed against the shingles. He rolled with the momentum, slowing as he slammed into a chimney. Pain shot along his back. Pieces of clay cracked beneath his weight. He scrambled to conceal himself as best he could, though the chimney was too narrow to do much. He sat, still, listening for anything that would suggest he had been discovered. After an unknown amount of time with only the sounds of the night reaching his ears he risked a look back to the wall. A trio of fur-cloaked guards stood close by. Kris tried to focus on their words when they came to him as clear as though they were speaking right beside him.

"I'm not saying you didn't hear what you heard, just that whatever it was it isn't here now."

"You're new, kid. Sound travels funny up here." said another. "Probably just some dogs nosing around." Someone patted the younger guard on the back, his chainmail jingling.

The third voice was less relaxed than the first two though a change was present. "You're probably right. Maybe I just need some sleep."

Laughter.

"The hours don't get any better." There were footsteps as the guards returned to their original posts.

Kris allowed himself to breathe normally. This new trick came to him with relative ease. He sat for a few minutes switching in and out of it until he felt confident he had it down.

The distance to the wall was greater than the first jump and higher. The guard was about to turn for another circuit, leaving an opening. It had to be now. Kris rounded the chimney and took a few steps back before running. He knew from the battle that he was stronger. He just wished that he had not waited until now to find out how much. The roof passed beneath him in long strides, his feet light in spite of his speed. He let his cloak fall. Once he landed he would need to be ready to defend himself and it would only get in the way. Kris came to the edge and pushed off. The ground fell away. His arm was outstretched, reaching for the lip of the wall. Instead of falling short as he expected, Kris kept rising. The force propelling him upwards was more than he expected. Stone collided with his chest as his chin whipped down onto the ledge. Blood filled his mouth. His arms slapped against the concrete but held, stopping him as he started to slide. Dots of light spotted his vision. He kept his grip tight until everything cleared and pulled himself up. Only luck saved him from the spear that came down.

The guard was younger than Kris and his blow was slow, off target. His eyes were wide, his breaths rapid. He adjusted the grip on his spear and struck again. Kris saw the attack seconds before it came and rolled aside, sweeping the guard's legs out with his own. The knife was in his hand and at the boy's throat before he could make a sound.

Weak limbs tried feebly to pry Kris' arm away. He pushed down on the knife, drawing blood. The boy stopped struggling. Kris held his life beneath that steel. It would be easy. Just like the others. He lifted the boy's head and forced it back down onto the stone. Kris would be gone when he woke. With any luck the headache would overthrow any memory of him.

He moved the guard's unconscious body further down the wall and glanced around. There was a training field on the ground below, wooden dummies with swords and shields grouped beside rows of archery targets. The multi-colored rings were torn where arrows had struck. A barracks stood at the far side, sharing the wall with a stable. There were a handful of men guarding the area. More gathered by a pair of fire pits by the keep. He counted a dozen more on the walls. Everything he saw he wrote down, sketching out certain spots as best he could. Maia would want all that he could bring back.

Lights shimmered in the topmost window of the keep. There was breeze tonight. A figure moved past, his body cloaked in shadow. Even at this distance Kris could see that the man was wearing robes too fine to belong to some military officer. Adding the fact that he was in the highest room... *The baron.* The man had been the focus of every loss and hardship suffered by the elves and here he was, just yards away. Kris read the history books. He knew the change the war underwent once Gerold took power. The former baron had been actively trying to pull Falhofna away from this bloodshed. He had even made some progress. Kris felt his hand rest on the leather grip of his knife. The people here had to be tired of the war as well. Their children were the ones being handed a spear and told to fight. They were not soldiers. *How many children had been sent south? How many would not return?* If the baron had kids like these guarding his walls, his situation had to be desperate. Now was the perfect time. This was why Maia sent him, though she never came out and said it. She wanted information, yes, but what she wanted more was Gerold's head.

And Kris had a chance to give that to her. As long as he could get past the guards. There were too many for him to take on his own. If he could wield magick in the way Feltahn had, then maybe. But as it was he had only the blade at his thigh against axes and swords. *Maybe I could get one of their weapons, even those odds at least.* He jostled the idea around for a minute or so before squashing it. There were too many. He needed another way in.

A second figure joined the baron by the window. He was taller, thin, but Kris cared little about that. It was the ears that he could not avert his focus from. They were elven. He nearly fell back, his balance lost for a moment. Such a thing was unthinkable. There were elves who sought peace and were willing to forgive the past to achieve it but none who would be found in the baron's personal chambers. None who would do the things necessary to earn that level of trust. The only turncoats in the whole of the war were hung by the Falhofnans after selling out the last of their secrets. It had proven the length of their generosity. All that meant was whoever this elf was, he knew enough to convince Gerold that he was still worth much more alive. Kris needed to find out what that was.

The distance was too great to hear what they were saying even with his newfound ability, forcing him to try and get closer. Too many men at the gate. No vantage point. He huddled where he hid the boy in no better a situation than before. Only now his urgency was increased. He wrote down what he could make of the elf and continued along the wall. The patrols would notice that the boy was not in his place and the keep would lock itself down. Kris would have no chance of getting in after that.

The crenulations hid him well enough while he was on the other side of them but here he was not so fortunate. Kris moved quickly but casually, timing his footsteps when the most backs were turned. He continued along this way until he noticed the guard still unconscious against the stone. He had come full around without even noticing. It was hopeless. The keep was impossible to penetrate in his present circumstances. There was no other way into the keep aside from the chimney and since he had no way of reaching that either the book he brought would have to be enough. He struck the bottom of his fist down onto the stone. *Tell me.* He turned at the sound of boot steps, already too late. Steel was in hand.

"Stay where you are." He kept the point of his sword leveled against Kris, sure of his position before shouting back to his fellow. "Is he still alive?"

"Aye, though he'll have a nasty bump when he wakes." the other man said.

"You're lucky for that much. But assaulting a soldier...." The guard grinned, shaking his head as he spoke.

Kris batted the sword aside with his forearm and gripped the man's throat with his other hand. The blade *clanged* off the top of the wall before falling into the dark below. Kris squeezed harder and brought his fist around. The soldier hit the stone as his friend reacted, barreling full-force into Kris' chest. They landed in a heap of punches and kicks, rolling as each tried to get the edge over the other. Kris tasted blood as the Falhofnan's elbow connected with his jaw. He returned with a quick knee that took the guard's breath. Neither of them noticed the stairs.

They separated as they fell, bouncing against the hard edges. Kris rolled over onto his back as he hit the dirt. He arched up and pulled a rock away before lying flat again. Each breath caused him to wince. One of his ribs was broken. He tried to stand when his leg refused to bend, sending him back down. The guard was not far away and looked to have similar difficulty closing the distance. Kris fought off some of his dizziness enough to look around. They had landed in the courtyard. The door to the keep was facing him. As was the dozen or so soldiers who stood in a half-circle before them. Hands moved for their weapons while others looked on, confusion written across their faces. More were coming over as well. The notebook was still in his pack. It hadn't come loose in the fall. He had to get up, to get out of here.

"What's this then?" one said.

"It's Charlie." another said as he ran to the fallen Falhofnan. "You alright?"

Charlie took a moment to answer and grabbed at his shoulder, holding back a shout. "Think my arm's broken. Keep your blades on that one. He already hit Jakob and may have killed Reynor too."

Whatever doubts the others may have had were wiped away then. Swords were drawn and spears raised. The soldier helped Charlie to his feet. Kris pushed himself up enough to put his back to the wall. The first soldier to speak moved with his sword lowered and Kris started working through the best way to counter the likeliest strike. A few would die but not enough. He would fall as well. He angled his hand, creating a clear path for his dagger. Sweat coated his palms and invited a chill. His hand started to shake. *A few steps closer.*

The air turned unnaturally cold. Kris kept his eyes on the soldier's sword arm when the others watching went quiet. The guard turned and his body stiffened. Charlie tried his best to stand on his own strength but couldn't. The men were too thickly packed for Kris to see behind. "Well. What's going on here?" It was the elf, Kris knew. The voice could not belong to any man. "It must be of great importance, seeing that it brought so many of you from your posts."

The crowd was larger than Kris first thought, consisting of more than just those by the keep. There was no way he could have fought through them all. A gap formed as the soldiers moved to either side, allowing the elf to pass. He was paler than he ought to have been with robes of blue and grey draped over his thin frame. Cold surrounded him.

"Who's this?" the elf asked.

Charlie responded. "We caught him trying to come over the wall – me and Reynor."

He gave no acknowledgement. "Why would you want to do a thing like that? Thievery? I was told enough of your ilk were executed after the coup to dissuade any others." He looked over Kris as though he was studying a text. "No, that's not it. I suppose it doesn't matter seeing that they're going to hang you." He turned to speak with the nearest officer when Kris felt it.

The magick was stirring. *Could've picked a better time.* Kris could see what was previously hidden from him laid out across his mind. All he needed to do was mold it.

The elf turned back cutting off his own words as his eyes shone almost white. *Could he tell? Was that possible?* Kris put his questions aside and instead threw the full weight of his will. The stone at his back trembled. Cracks began to form. The elf rushed towards him as the first brick burst free. It clipped his shoulder, spinning him around and continuing into the chest of the soldier behind him. More flew forward with a chorus of thunder. Men dove to the ground and tried running. Stones found nearly a dozen of them, killing a few while others were laid low. It bought Kris time.

He felt each blow as though it was he who was throwing them. His body could barely stand. Rest. He needed rest. But not yet. The magick was directed toward himself. Pain raced up his leg but it was too late to stop. He clenched back a scream, exhaling as it faded. The stiffness was gone. Nausea gripped him and his vision swam as he pulled himself to his feet. His ribs would have to wait. He took deep breaths and drew his dagger. The elf was up as well, showing no signs of the fear that held the others. Dust clouded the air but through it, Kris would have sworn he was smiling.

Air turned to ice in the elf's hand. "I can help you. Show you things that gnome never would have dreamed of."

Feltahn. Kris clenched his fist over the hilt of his dagger. If he knew about Feltahn…. The men started to regain their original composure, retrieving their fallen weapons to stand beside the elf. As much as he wanted to fight, to beat answers out of this traitor, he knew that road was closed to him. His limbs were exhausted and could not sustain combat for long. Any offensive magick like his work with the wall was out of the question. *What, then?* His hand brushed against his pocket and the answer became clear.

The elf struggled with his words, forcing them out. The blade in his hand tapped against his hip repeatedly. "I will not offer this again, boy," the elf said. His smile was waning.

In answer Kris threw his dagger towards the elf and pulled the wooden stag free. There was not much left in him but as he began directing the magick as he wished that pressure lessened. The more he urged it on the simpler it became, the path opening before him. Kris ducked out of the way of the elf's own projectile and rolled forward. The stag was growing. He took shelter behind one of the archery targets as two more shards of ice struck its back. Legs kicked as the wood was filled with life. Kris felt his heart race. He didn't expect it to work, yet here it was. The connection was easier to maintain while a steady flow coursed through him.

Boots stamped across the dirt. In a few seconds they would be on him. The stag reached the size of a small horse and was still growing. It would have to do. Kris climbed on its back and spurred it forward with his heels. Shouts chased after him as he gained speed. Blades of ice left blue streaks in the air as they passed. Blood dripped down his neck as a cut opened. He angled the stag around the stables for the flight of stairs he knew to be behind it. Horses shied away as they rounded the corner. A pair of Falhofnans did the same. Kris only had to think it and the stag lowered its head, knocking one to the side with its antler. The other landed a blow with his axe that took a chunk of wood from its thigh. It made no noise or sound of pain and kept moving.

The sky line opened up overhead, the city stretching out before him. A chill crept up Kris' back. He did not have to look to know the elf was getting closer. He kicked the stag into motion. It ran straight to the edge of the wall and before Kris could stop it they were in the air. They leapt higher than he would have thought it capable of and landed on the rooftop across from the wall. The impact jarred him and threatened to throw him from his mount but he hung on. He risked a look back to see the elf standing at the wall. His face was flat, void of emotion. Kris was not sure what he feared more.

His body ached. The throbbing in his head was even worse. They had escaped the city and kept running until only trees surrounded them. Sleep beckoned him and he very nearly gave in. *He mentioned Feltahn.*

4

"We should have heard from him by now." Thysilar said. His health had improved enough over the past week that the physicians harassed him less for leaving their roof. Walking, it turned out, was the limit of their generosity. It did not stop him from carrying his blade. A bowstring snapped as it was released and Muriel's arrow took flight. The tip struck the straw dummy center mass, joining a dozen or so others. Halfar watched disinterestedly as she restrung another. He had been cleaning his blades and moved on to his armor. Others around them were doing the same. "How long can a simple scouting mission take?"

"He went into the city. There's nothing simple about that." Muriel said.

"Assuming the boy even survived." Halfar said, not looking up. "It's a dangerous road that better soldiers walked and died on."

Thysilar toyed with the hilt of his sword. He had known Kris as a boy, trained him as best he could, given Estelle's concerns. If they were talking about that boy he would have shared Halfar's thoughts. Thysilar never would have let him leave. But after what he saw outside The Pine, everything he heard about from the fighting inside… This was not the Kris he knew as a boy. He could handle himself. Yet still Thysilar felt on edge. *I should be there with him. Not trapped here.* In the days since Kris left, the elves had been busy preparing the defenses. An army would be coming. They did not plan on fighting here, but if Kris did not return in time, or if what he found was not sufficient then their options were few. Thysilar slid the sword in and out of its scabbard. *I should be out there with him.*

"I'd say he's shown enough to give him more credit than you're showing." Muriel said as she let another arrow fly. The quiver by her feet was empty and she went over to retrieve the shafts from the dummy.

"Not to me. Or you." Halfar said, directing his words at Muriel. "All we have is the rumor of soldiers. You know as well as I that under duress it is easy for the mind to get carried away."

Muriel shrugged her acknowledgement, returning the arrows to their place.

"I saw it." Thysilar said.

"Half-dying and bleeding from a dozen wounds?"

The hilt of the sword *clacked* against its sheath. "I saw it." Thysilar repeated.

Halfar looked up from his work to meet Thysilar's words. He remained stern, unfazed.

"He gained Maia's trust. That could not have been from nothing." Muriel said, doing her best to calm the two elves. Even those amongst the inner circle were not immune to gossip. Not with magick.

"Desperation can inspire many things."

"Only if the mind is weak. Is that what you are accusing me of, Halfar?" All three turned at the woman's voice. Maia was dressed in riding clothes, leather pants with a vest over a matching brown shirt. She had her hair down with her red cloak clasped about her shoulders. "These are desperate days, I agree. Days where it doesn't hurt to have faith."

How she knew his name neither of them could guess. Thysilar expected to feel something… more, being in the company of one with Maia's history. She had been fighting since their first encounter with the humans, when trade and peace masked the truth. It could be argued that she, along with the rest of her family, were the only reason the elves had any semblance of civilization left to them.

"I have plenty of faith, my lady." Halfar responded. "I believe if magick ever was to return it would not be in the hands of a human." He stood and rested his armor over his shoulder before leaving.

Muriel moved to follow him but Maia stopped her. "It's alright. I remember being told as a child to 'take it all in.' My father had brought my brother and me to Tier' Nahl. We had never seen anything like it, not in our village. It was a reminder of what our people lost and were not like to see again. When the humans came I thought it all made sense. The world was changing, ushering our people out for this younger race." She smiled at a joke known only to her. "You could say my opinions have changed."

"Still, it's hard to believe that magick would return and choose Kris as its vessel." Muriel said. "Nothing against him, of course." She directed the second half to Thysilar but he took no offense.

It was not the first time the thought had entered his mind. Since Kris saved him that day outside The Pine he felt something changed. Even before that, when the wolves should have torn the pair of them apart. Aside from saying he was safe, Estelle refused to speak on the subject. He sensed the same now. He doubted Maia knew much more but there was still something. And he was growing tired of secrets. There was not enough time for him to question Kris about it himself before he left. Everything was moving fast and he was not in the mindset of being left behind. Whatever may be coming. "Have you heard anything yet?"

"No." Maia said plainly. "Their army is still on its way."

That much he had been able to discern for himself. "What of Kris' plan?"

The elven commander sat on the stool Halfar had been using, a water skin in her hand. She took a long draught. "Your wounds are healing well?" she asked, wiping a few drops from her lips and chin. "The Bear was no small foe. Dozens of others did not stand up nearly so well."

Even with his experience, all his training, The Bear had Thysilar beat. "I've always preferred a bow over a sword."

"Even so, you're not without a good measure of skill."

Thysilar waited for her to continue, speaking when he felt she wasn't. "Is there a point to all this?" Muriel let the bowstring go slack in her hands, the arrow barely held between her fingertips.

Maia looked over to him with the same level of warmth she'd had since the conversation started. "This 'boy' you seem to remember so well returns from over a year spent in the mountains, seemingly with full knowledge of the battle, kills Berengar, and brings what's left of The Pine to its knees. I didn't know him before but I doubt he would've been capable of that before he disappeared." She pulled the string of her bracelet, turning it so the pair of beads were on top. "I don't know what happened when magick left our people. But having heard the stories, seen some of those things firsthand, is it so difficult to believe that it's found a way back?"

184

The training yard emptied as the watches were rotated, eventually leaving Thysilar with the archery range to himself. Maia had left to oversee the defenses, allowing her words to sit. But not before telling him to make sure his scouts were ready. He had his old command back. He was unaware of the weight that had settled on his shoulders until it was lifted.

Stiffness settled in his legs. After a few minutes he was able to work past it. His fingers slid along the edge of a bow leaning against the post in front of him. *It'll be back to the shadows. To the quiet.* With his eyes closed he took a deep breath, filling his lungs with the fresh scent of oak and elm and fallen leaves. There was a dampness in the air. He took up the bow with three swift moves, falling to one knee as he reached for an arrow. Pain settled along his back and leg and threatened to overwhelm him. Maybe he did need to rest. He had been so used to being the one there when Kris got into trouble, either to discipline or, at times, help him get out of it.

It was no secret what Thysilar thought of the humans, Kris included, at least during the earlier years of his life. He was still surprised by it now, looking back. *There was a time where I would've watched him leave with a smile. Let the humans kill each other. What did it matter?* His first shot missed wide, jutting awkwardly from the edge of the target. He clenched his fist and held it for a minute or so before releasing. It still trembled but control was returning. The next shot was closer, if still a miss.

Kris' plan was still in motion. All they were waiting for was his return, the information he volunteered to gather. And he'll do it. Maia was right and she had only known him for a few hours. The things Thysilar saw him do should have been more than enough to convince himself as well.

It took two quivers before he hit his mark.

The fort settled down some once night came. As important as the defenses were, rest took precedent. It did not matter how well-fortified a position was if those defending it were too tired to even hold a bow. A few not on watch still walked the square or sat by fires. Berengar had a generous supply of wine casks in the storeroom and Aelen made sure those who fought were the first to choose their share. As of yet they remained civil with little outlandish behavior. Thysilar walked past a few groups huddled around their barrel before coming up to his scouts.

They were minor compared to those connected to Aelen and Maia's forces, never looking more like the militia that they were. Thysilar cared little about that. Their blades were still sharp, their bows strong. *Each elf here has bled for one another. What more do I need?*

Movement by the gate caught his attention and he changed his path away from his scouts. The elves atop the wall attempted to keep their voices low but were not doing too well. Something was coming through the trees. It could not have been the Falhofnans. An army would struggle to make such timing on open ground, let alone in heavily wooded terrain between the city and The Pine. Their scouts? Thysilar shook away the question as soon as he heard it. He knew their scouts. They were men that would never allow themselves to be discovered by a night watch. Another thought came to him then. A hope. He knew he was right as soon as it entered his mind, unexplainable but assuring. "Open the gate." Faces were blank, their eyes displaying their confusion. "Open it!"

Thysilar was already on the ground as the great wooden doors were pulled open. He walked through while they were still in motion. Kris stepped into the open clearing at the front of the fort, climbing down from a stag missing one of its antlers. It was one of the largest he had seen, its appearance bringing other questions that faded when he saw the bundle of cloth lying across the back of the stag. He knew what it covered. He had seen too many.

A breeze stirred the cloth in his arms, revealing a glimpse of gray hair. Kris said nothing as he approached, his bloodshot eyes unblinking.

5

Estelle's feet sank slowly with each step into the wet soil. Dampness clung to her clothes and an unshakeable cold had settled in her bones. The burial was short, attended by only a few. Estelle doubted even that much would have taken place without Kris' insistence. He wanted to take him back up to the mountain but Maia would not allow it. Not with the information Kris had brought back. Time was too precious.

They found an alcove at the foot of the mountain and laid the gnome's body to rest. No words were said. No big gestures. Kris sealed the opening behind them, marking the stone with an image of the Tree. She expected tears to come when the elves had approached her door. And again when she saw Kris sitting by Feltahn's still form. *He promised me. After all these years, all the pain and death, he promised me.*

"How are you doing?" Kris asked. The rest of the group had moved ahead of her as thoughts of the past slowed her steps without her knowledge. Kris walked by her side, for how long she was unsure. A cloak of heavy furs was draped over his shoulders as the weather continued its descent.

"I'm fine, dear. These old bones have seen worse winters than this is like to be." Estelle said. She kept as much of her usual warmth as she could but Kris was unreadable. When he was younger she prided herself on being able to tell when he was upset with little more than a shift in his eyes. "Though they wouldn't mind a rest." she added. The gravesite was half a day's walk from the fort with a steady pace, something she was able to keep up with throughout the journey's first leg.

"You don't have to pretend anymore. I'm not a child. Feltahn told me about his life before he was chosen. The parts about you." For a moment his face softened. "Why didn't you tell me?"

"He had no right," Estelle said. She stopped walking and forced Kris to do the same.

He looked down at her as he spoke, never looking more like a man grown. "You're my mother. Over twenty years you've taken care of me, did what you thought best to raise me into the man I am now. You should have been the one to tell me about your life before that cabin."

"He had no –" Estelle started to say.

"You had no right!" Kris said. "You took me as your own, raised me like a son, yet you kept this from me for so many years."

Estelle was taken aback by the sudden intensity but the feeling did not last long. "I did what I needed to keep you safe. It was dangerous enough having a human living amongst our people after all they've done to us. The risks I was taking… It was for the best."

"Keeping me in the dark? Lying to me?"

"I never lied to you." Estelle answered back without pause. "Everything I've done was my own choice and for my own reasons.

188

I don't have to explain any of them to you." Kris stared long at her without a word and barely a motion aside from the steady rhythm of his breathing. He was too upset for this one secret to be the reason. She was not the one he wanted to be fighting with. "I miss him."

His eyes changed at that.

"He came to me the day you left. He wanted to start over, find some place far away to settle down. Just him and me. No one else. I should have said yes. The gods know I wanted to." *But I didn't*. A single snowflake rested on her cheek, melting almost instantly. There was something he hadn't told her. A reason for him to be so upset. It would be pointless to ask him, she knew. He had his walls up now.

"I know who did it." Kris said, his voice teetering on a whisper.

Estelle didn't need to ask what the 'who' pertained to. When she first heard that Feltahn had died she did not think that much on how. Gnome's enjoyed a life longer than many just as hers, and he had lived long past that already. *The magick had kept him alive as long as it needed him. Just as it will do to Kris.* "How?"

"He recognized it in me back at the castle. Until I tapped into it he was going to let them kill me. If he recognized it in me then he would've sensed it back with Feltahn as well." Kris said, his eyes staring at something just behind Estelle.

"He knew there would be dangers and accepted that." Estelle said. "This is not on your shoulders." She had been playing that conversation over in her mind the last few days and could still hear his voice. It was for that reason he pushed her away. How could he be expected to do what he needed while fearing for her safety as well? *I could have given him an argument.* Yet she didn't. "We all make our choices."

"And he made his." Kris said.

Estelle only nodded. She did not think he was referring to the gnome. Her hand found his and squeezed tightly. Kris let it stay for a few seconds before moving away.

"You should think about leaving."

"I was planning on it, maybe stay a night or two before finding someone kind enough to offer me a carriage home. Don't expect it'll be long before she has you starting for the castle." The soldiers had that anxiety about them. It would be soon.

"That's not what I mean." Kris said, looking ahead to the others. They noticed they were two short and stopped, taking the time to rest. "I'm not sure how, but this elf has power. Similar to mine only he knows how to wield it. He's already shown how far he's willing to go to get to me and I can't risk him finding you."

"You can't put that on yourself. I'm not a child. For many years I've lived in these woods, keeping myself and my kids safe, and I plan on doing so for many years to come."

"I'm going to kill him. The baron. Everyone who tries to stop me. If it doesn't turn out the right way there'll be an army out here, angry, and with nothing between them and every elven village they can find. Please."

There was a serious note to his tone she had not heard before. Anger was ruling him now. *And it will see him through. Worrying about me will only hold him back.* "I have a few friends by the coast."

Kris leaned over to kiss her forehead. "Thank you."

Estelle gripped his forearm, saying nothing else. She watched him rejoin the others before wiping the moisture from her face. A shiver wracked her body as a cold wind blew by, kicking up fallen leaves and sending those still attached to their limbs to the ground. *What happened on that mountain?* She knew the answer as soon as the thought was finished. It was the same thing that happened to Feltahn so many years before. *But his fate does not belong to Kris. Not my son.* He stood a head taller than the rest and it was clear that they viewed him… differently. To them he represented both the past and future. Estelle knew him as the child, clutching his blanket as snow piled around him. *He would kill the baron and this elf, as he promised. Not because Maia or anyone else asked him, but because he* wanted *to.*

The faintest smile broke Estelle's still face. It wasn't snowing.

6

"Leave." Gerold said.

"It's been weeks since we supped together," Letta replied plainly. She sliced off a piece of roast duck and brought it to her mouth as though the words were enough.

The baron turned away from the door to rest his gaze on his wife. "Now."

Letta stared back, unflinching as she chewed. Her fork rang out against the long walls of the empty dining hall. She wiped a drop of grease from her chin and stood, letting the cloth fall as she walked to the door. "He's yours."

Jak allowed her to push past him before taking her seat. For the first time since Gerold had known him the elf appeared ragged. He wore his usual blues but the clothes lacked their previously held luster, blemished with wrinkles and dark stains. *He's been sleeping in them.* Then he noticed the heavy bags under Jak's eyes, the loose strands of hair hanging about his face. *Or not at all.*

"This is quite the meal." Jak said, his mouth half-full with a generous bit of bread. He finished chewing barely a second before finishing Letta's near-empty wineglass. A satisfied groan passed his lips. "It's been decades since I had a vintage as good as this. I can see why you married her."

Gerold watched as the elf cleared half the plate and reach for another biscuit, but not before refilling the wine. For the moment it appeared he was content to simply sit there and eat. *It's as though his outburst in the courtyard never happened.* He had been sitting in his study, going over the books Jak had brought him, when he heard the shouts. Assassins were nothing new. The early years of his barony had seen to that. *The guilds learned fast.* But to see Jak's reaction, the power he possessed in full display.... It could not have been something so casual. And that was not the only question he wanted answered. "If I'd known you came here to eat I would've had more prepared."

Jak ignored him and poured more wine.

"Are you planning to tell me where you've been these past days? In case you haven't noticed, time is not among our list of assets."

Silence, save for the crunch of bone as Jak tore into a leg of duck.

Gerold swiped his hand out across the table, knocking his glass as well as those plates and bowls closest to the floor, gaining the elf's attention. Jak stopped chewing and looked up from his plate. "Oh good," Gerold said, "You're still listening. For a moment I thought you'd forgotten about our arrangement." There was no anger in the elf's face, his expression indifferent. "A man scales my walls and kills my men. I'm no fool. I know that no small measure of the city's unrest is directed towards me. Such things are to be expected in times of war. What concerns me is when this would-be assassin draws you out the way he did. To show such strength…. It would appear you haven't been completely honest with me."

"The books I gave you were not easy to come across. Their previous owners took great pride in their collections. You would be amazed by the lengths they had gone to guarantee their protection." Jak dabbed at a drop of wine spilling down his chin. "To them those words were stories, written down by men long dead to forewarn their progeny of past mistakes. History as the great teacher. Their value lie in their rarity. Nothing more. They are not made as you and I. We know better." He pushed his chair back and stood. "Come with me."

The halls of the keep were uncommonly quiet, a fact Gerold had made note of once the elf's power was revealed. *They're afraid of him. And me. Perhaps they should be.* Meals were served and taken in their quarters. There was no one to bar their path.

"We've both heard stories about magick. Why it left, where it went. I'd bet every servant in these walls has heard it too, in one variation or another. If we believed as they do we would not have arrived where we are now." Jak guided him through his own keep as though he was the guest, not its lord. They turned past the kitchens and the main banquet hall, heading toward the sparring grounds. "You believed the magick was still here and you meant to find it. That single goal brought you your title. It's fueled your every action. To have such surety in life is a rare thing. There is nothing quite like it." He stopped at the door and placed his hands on Gerold's shoulder, staring down into his eyes. "That is what I felt when I saw the boy. My whole life I searched for what now flows through his veins."

"It was here?" Gerold asked. How many men had died scouring the forest? For years he kept the king's demands at bay, weathered the countless letters and pressure from the other barons. *After all of that, it ends up at my door.* "And you let it escape?"

194

"Do not misread my calm demeanor, baron. He caught me unaware, a luxury he will not receive twice." Jak pushed open the heavy oaken door. "After you."

The air was crisp with little wind. A handful of men stood in the yard, a crimson falcon embroidered on their chest. Anton's scouts. Their veteran commander was present at the center, his confusion plainer than he'd cared to show. They were not what Gerold was drawn to.

Circling the yard was a pair of hounds, though he struggled calling them that. In the dark between the torches they were barely more than an outline, only visible by their breath, frosting the air. As they moved closer to the firelight he saw that his first guess was only right in the most basic sense. Their hides were made of pure ice. Light reflected off each angle, revealing rows of teeth sharp as blades. Empty eyes stared at him alone.

"What are they?" Gerold asked. The elf wanted him to see this. Anton as well.

"They're part of the reason I've been away. The spells required to give them life were more complex than I had thought. They left me weak, for a time." Jak crouched down and reached out to one of his pets. It nuzzled his hand and nipped playfully at him before continuing along its route.

It explained the elf's absence and appearance true enough, but there was yet another question it did not. "Why? They're formidable to be sure, but I saw your power, the things you can do. There can't be many still alive who could contend with it." Gerold had known since that first night in his study that there was more to Jak than his meager appearance would lead others to believe. *But to see it with my own eyes was something entirely different.*

"Though my hounds can hold their own that is not their purpose." Jak said, his eyes following the beast as it went. "It's regrettable that the boy got away. However, his escape bore unexpected fruit." He rose too fast for Gerold to react and pushed his palm against the baron's chest. A cold unlike any he had experienced gripped his lungs. Jak held him up as his body weakened. "Blood. It was not much, but more than was required for them to get the scent. When he gets the message I left for him he will come. All I need to do is wait." The hounds had stopped their pacing and stood side-by-side, slowly moving closer. "You shared my drive, had the manpower to cover more ground than I could myself. It could even be argued that if it wasn't for your fiendish reputation the boy would never have been drawn out. For that, you have my gratitude."

A single tear streaked down the baron's face, freezing before it could reach his cheek. The ice began to spread, sapping every ounce of strength he had left. Was his judgment so clouded? All he could see was the power, the things he could accomplish with it. Peace would finally be achieved along the border villages. Falhofna would at last become the beacon it was always meant to be. *That was worth every life lost and more.*

None of it mattered now, of course.

He looked to Anton and his men but all they did was watch. Some glanced to one another, their hands hovering over the hilts of their blades or the shafts of their bows. But none moved to his aid. Not without their commander's word. Jak released him. The ground rose up faster than it ought to have. He felt nothing. His body had gone numb.

Jak brought his focus to Anton. "I imagine you're wondering why you were asked here."

Anton said nothing.

"The soldiers respect you. You'll be able to guarantee this transition moves smoothly, without any added bloodshed."

"And what transition would that be?" Anton asked. He was able to remain calm in front of the elf but Gerold had known him long enough to pick up on the subtle tells he refused to acknowledge. The scout's hands were kept by his sides. Still and unwavering. He was anxious, but in control. His body ready no matter the state of his mind.

"New leadership can be fickle, difficult for the people to accept. Riots, rebellion, knives waiting in the dark," Jak turned to the baron with eyes colder than the fingers stealing the life from him. "History as the great teacher."

The scout was unreadable. *Kill him.* Gerold willed. His breaths came labored, each harder than the last. There would be no saving himself. It was a hard truth, but there it was. Everything was numb, frozen from within. Sounds were muffled. His eyesight started to fade. *But I can still watch this bastard die. Kill him.*

"There are a few knights who would give you trouble. They were with him when he took power, made sure his path was clear." Anton did not look down. "They'll be at the pub by now, either the Quilted Stocking or the Stag's Head. I can have them rounded up by morning."

Jak's mouth twisted into a grin. "Very good. Keep it quiet. No witnesses."

Anton turned and said something to his men too faint for Gerold to hear. The yard cleared save for him and Jak. *He's gone, then.* The cold spread faster. Gerold's surroundings blurred but he could still make out the blue, piercing through the smog like some beacon, guiding home ships at sea. It was quiet. A wind blew, rustling the leaves of the trees beyond the wall. Niklas had shown trust, had welcomed Gerold in the same way he had with Anton. *Did he feel the same when he saw me at his door?* He never gave much thought to the baron he killed. *Who else could have done what I have?* Darkness spread. Silence consumed him, muting the hungry growls growing closer. *It had to be me.*

7

Said aloud he could see why the elves were hesitant to go along with him. He had barely begun to grasp control of the magick within him and the plan he drew up would require more. *Much more.* The decision had not been unanimous. Faelyn disagreed, of course. His distrust of Kris' power had been evident since they first met, and having hundreds of lives depending solely on its success pushed him past the edge of tolerance. If not for Aelen's backing the captain may have gone so far as to pull his troops from the battle altogether. Kris tried not to let the doubts fester, but he was hard-pressed to keep them all at bay. Not when they were doubts he himself shared.

"Do you believe you can do this?" Maia had asked, silencing the words of the other assembled elves.

The answer came quickly despite the clouds in his mind. "Yes." It was decided then, replacing 'how' with 'where'. The Falhofnan army was still working its way toward them, with each day bringing them closer. Maia wanted the elves battle ready by the week's end. *She wanted* me *ready.* The elves had found their weapon. Saw a chance to put an end to this war. *And they were going to do whatever they could to exploit it.*

All work previously being done on the fort's defenses was stopped, their focus shifted to the coming battle. Kris was given full reign to oversee it all. He had drawn up the plans as best he could and made sure the officers knew what needed to be done. Any wood required was taken from the fortifications. It was not as though they were needed anymore. "One day it's build, the next, tear down." one of the elves said. He was older than most with the years showing their passage on his tired face. His hair was gray and thinning, leaving a pallet of bald skin atop his head. Olliver, his name was. "I hope you're sure this time."

Kris studied the parchment in his hands. It was a simple enough design. Nothing the elves could not handle. Magick or no, they maintained their talent for craftsmanship. "Just see that it's done right."

Olliver nodded and waved him off, speaking under his breath. He could say whatever he wanted about Kris. The job would get done.

"You seem to have stepped into the leadership role relatively well." Thysilar said. He wore his red cloak over leather armor, the hilt of his sword poking through. "Never would have expected that."

The group of elves started to apply Kris' changes as he turned to face the scout. Seeing Thysilar as he was brought him back nearly twenty years, when Kris was a boy and eager to see their red cloaks in person. Thysilar's was as worn now as it was that day, a few new tears aside. "Kind of just happened. You look better."

"Well enough. There's still a few days left."

"So you'll be joining us then." Regardless of what the physicians recommended, his mind was made. There would be no altering that.

"They don't have much of a choice. If she wants my cloaks, she takes me at their head. And from what I've heard, this plan you've thought up calls for every sword and bow you can find." Thysilar circled one of the finished crates the elves were told to dismantle and readjust. They could not afford to be off by even a thumb's length.

He's right. I need him. It could be done without his elves. There were thousands all around him to fill their role. But it was not just soldiers he needed. Not for this. Everyone had their part.

"So we'll be brought through the gates in these?" Thysilar asked. He looked down at the growing rows of crates, wearing his doubt like a mask.

Kris tucked the parchment within his cloak and watched as Olliver shouted orders to a group of elves dismantling the palisades nearby. What they were meant to defend against he did not know, but it mattered little now. "Something like that."

The elf chuckled. "They're not exactly spacious. Can't hold more than two, and that's being generous."

"I've worked the numbers. Cramped, yes, but they'll serve. Besides, it won't be for too long. You'll have to trust me."

"I remember back when you were just a boy, how often you would say that to me. Trading Estelle's best mule for a bag of seeds. Deciding to leap off the highest peak into the lake. It got to the point where I started to doubt you even knew what the word meant."

"That seed was supposed to double our harvest after a month." Kris said, smiling as the memory took shape. How he believed that elf was speaking the truth, he did not know. *Young and gullible.*

Thysilar nodded, moving his fingertips along the wood of the box. "No one could say your heart was in the wrong place, even while your head was not." He paused after that, the corner of his mouth rising. "You had a look to your eyes, the same as now. However crazy the words coming out of your mouth, if I saw that look I went along with it."

"When I tried convincing you to help hunt that bear eating our livestock?"

"Most of the time." Thysilar said, letting his grin show.

"The bear's a little bigger this time." Kris said. Even after everything he had seen and done over the past year, talking to Thysilar made him feel as though time had not passed at all. He was still the wide-eyed child, eager for his older brother's approval.

"My elves are yours." Thysilar turned away from the yard and half-finished boxes. "Just bring them home."

The boy was gone again, replaced by the man. *The weapon.* Kris could feel the power stir inside him, sensing what was ahead. That was good. He needed its cooperation now.

8

The city was locked down with twice the number of men guarding the walls and gate. They were conscripts, fresh soldiers, their armor either too tight or hung loose across their shoulders. Blades were slung through belts without scabbards. Those fortunate enough to be given a helm were then faced with the issue of adjustment, tipping it this way and that to keep their vision clear. Kris was able to move past them without incident. Closer to the keep the patrols had increased. It changed nothing. The keep was not his target today.

It was just past midday but the roads were quiet. Men and women roamed the cobblestones, though the latter greatly outnumbered the former. Kris kept his hood up and pace relaxed, opting out of his red cloak for a less suspicious brown. Soldiers patrolled each block, hands on halberds that shone dully in the clouded sun. They were searching people seemingly at random, with a focus primarily on the men. There were likely those who managed to avoid the conscriptions. *They're looking for those they may have missed. Not too young, or old. Anyone like me.* He kept to the crowds as much as possible and the shadows when it was not.

The school house stood where he remembered, daylight revealing the host of cracks and pits marring its walls. Shingles were missing above, pieces of orange littering the ground around its base. *At least the door is still whole.* Kris pushed through the squealing to the sight of a dozen children, eyes staring through the sudden silence. Katarina stood beside a canvas map that took up more than half of the wall.

"Kris?" she asked. Her hand fell down by her side as, for a moment, her surroundings were forgotten. That fact returned quickly though and she turned back to her class. "I think you've heard me enough for one day. You have your notes, I expect you to study them and be ready for an examination tomorrow. That includes all of the eastern nations as well as their capitals." A chorus of moans and groans filled the room, accompanying the scraping of wood against wood as they pushed their chairs back to leave. There was no one to see them home but they seemed not to mind. Katarina waited for the room to clear, shutting the door behind the last child. "Didn't expect to see you again so soon. Or in my classroom."

"Sorry. I didn't mean to interrupt their history lesson." Kris said, walking over to the map. Feltahn had shown him one similar, albeit older, with many of the territories having changed hands either through conquest or politics. Elven maps were different still. To see the same lands divided and named a dozen different ways made little sense. *It's all a ruse. In the end the kings will die, as will their sons. What are titles to the passage of time?*

"It's alright. The way things have been going lately, their focus has been better. I feel lucky when half of my students show up." Katarina moved from desk to desk, collecting the quills and sealing the inkpots left open. She placed them down in her desk drawer and took the last bunch Kris brought over. "Thank you." Her eyes lingered on his. "So to what do I owe this pleasure?"

There would be no going back. Too much relied on her agreement. Considering its weight, she handled it well. "I know this is a lot to ask of you, but there's no one else here I can trust."

She sat at her desk staring down at a pile of papers stacked beside an open book, the words inside written by a neat hand. "That was you." she said almost too soft for Kris to hear. "You were the one who tried to kill the baron."

"I only went to get information, but I saw a chance. I had to take it."

"With no thought to what would happen to rest of us. This all started after that night. The drafts, patrols –."

"Those things and more were happening long before I came to this city. The baron's crimes are long and plenty." Kris cut in.

"Maybe, but at least then he knew when to stop. Now..." Her voice trailed off.

Nothing Kris said would do anything other than start an argument. *One neither of us need.* It was out there now, and up to her to decide. He could not disagree with all of her logic, though. What would happen once Gerold was killed? Most of the people would not accept an elf to rule and even if they did, no elf would want the role. One of their own would have to take that mantle. *They had been fighting for too long. How could anyone overcome that much bad blood?*

"Can you promise their safety?" She looked up at him for the first time since sitting down.

"Yes." Kris said.

Katarina walked around the desk, taking his hand in hers. "I know some folks that'll help. Might hate the baron about as much as you."

"How will I know them?"

"Just look for the candles." she said.

There it was. He knew he should have felt more, differently, yet he didn't. There was still work to be done. "Thank you." Without another word or hint he leaned in and brought her lips to his. The taste of peppermint filled his mouth and he wanted more. It masked the lie on his tongue. He broke the kiss, exhaling a deep breath to calm the beating in his chest. "Stay inside. Whatever you hear."

9

There was a quiet on the wall that left Anton unsettled. His own men were scattered, interspersed with regular soldiers all along the surrounding stonework. He kept a handful of his best close by. The baron's orders would be obeyed, but only so much as they needed to be. *Falcons were never meant to be used this way.* Before him the ground laid open and flat, from the base of the wall to the tree line. Already snow had blanketed most of it in white. *I should be out there.* He had lost count of the number of drafts. The new lord appeared to rival the last. *An army of boys and he holds back his men.* Even before he was given full command of the elite group of scouts he knew their role during the early years of the war.

Locate. Observe. Plot. Strike.

The tactics were successful then. *Before Niklas.* Gathering followers for a coup was not a difficult sell, if you knew where to look. And Anton did. *It seemed the gods had a sense of humor.*

Maps and officer reports dictated what needed to be done, not books filled with children's tales. His scouts were still hunting elves instead of chasing shadows. Anton had hoped once the knights were eliminated that Jak would see to restore the Falcons to their proper place. He pulled his wolfskin cloak tighter around his shoulders as the snow continued to fall. Winter had arrived.

A pair of scouts, Eckhart and Josef, stood beside a brazier along with four other soldiers. They were men Anton had known and fought beside for nearly ten years. Men who stood with him when Gerold came to their tent, a king's letter in hand. He would have them nowhere else. Eckhart was wiry, thin, with long limbs that made his cloak appear too large and out of place. Wisps of hair covered his face in a prepubescent beard. A trait that the aged scout heard about to no end. Josef was younger by nearly a decade and would have fit in among the ranks of knights. The leather and mail he wore were custom built to accommodate his added mass. Blonde hair spilled out from beneath his hood, appearing that much lighter so close to the fire.

"How long do you think this'll keep up?" Josef asked.

Eckhart shrugged, the act all but lost beneath his cloak. His hands were held out above the fire. "You know well enough how unpredictable the winters here can be. Wouldn't surprise me if the snows came straight until spring."

"It's the standing that makes it worse. A few more hours of this and my joints will be stiffer than the damn stones we're guarding."

Anton had to agree. He had forgotten what the cold was like on the wall. *How do these men tolerate it?* The soldiers he had dealt with since taking over the city's defenses had joked about bundling up but he paid them little mind. He was their elder by twenty years in cases. What could they tell him that he had not learned himself? *They're children.* He considered it lucky they did not have to rely on such soldiers before now. *Things keep moving as they have and that luck will be worthless.*

"Stones we have no place on." Josef said, "We're wasted here with this grunt work. Have the legion man the walls and us in their stead. Outnumbered and still we could deliver that damn fort to the elf's feet." He was speaking with a youthful pride but there was still some truth to his words. It did not matter now. The pieces were set and could not be called back.

Jak cared little for the elves at The Pine, waving Anton away when he tried to bring the issue up to the new baron. None of it would matter, he had said. "Keep the gates barred." And so he did. *Ever the loyal soldier.*

"There's talk of war among the eastern lords. Both sides willing to pay good coin for skilled mercenaries."

Eckhart kept his head tilted down, his eyes hidden beneath his hood. "You'd be swinging by your neck before you cleared the border."

"All depends where you crossed." Anton looked up to see his men staring at him. Was that aloud? He had been drawn to the fire, watching as the flames started to spread slowly, charring the bark along its surface. Even as the fire grew he could not get warm. *Had he felt the same?*

"Sir?" Josef asked, wearing his confusion for all to see.

Eckhart pushed his hood back, the air brushed his matted down hair as it pleased.

He had been silent for too long. "This city isn't what it was when we first came here. I know you can see it as well as I, Eckhart. A disease has festered here, unchecked for too long. A disease that's already spread too far."

"The crown?" Eckhart asked.

There was much Anton had learned over the past years, more so the further Gerold fell into his quest. *Fool's errand, more like.*

Most of the letters were burned but not all. And the few he was able to get his hands on told him enough. He had advised Gerold against it in the early years, tried to push him towards ending the war first. His words would have been better suited to the baron's predecessor, all the good they had done. "With too many stops along the way."

If Eckhart was thrown by the news he gave no sign. He had been a soldier all his life, a Falcon for most of that. Politics were not unfamiliar to him. It was Josef who appeared the most put off, if for only a moment. It did not take long for his mind to turn back to profit.

"I have a cousin who works on a trade ship along the Dhalish coast. The captain's honest but he could be persuaded. My cousin is well-liked there."

"It's a long way from here to Dhal." Eckhart said. "And not cheap."

The Falcons were his. Anton would not force anyone but knew that aside from a handful, they would elect to follow. *What future could they find here?* Once news of the sorcerer's coup reached the capital it would be a matter of time before the tromp of Falhofnan boots were heard coming down from the north. The barons would lend their support, of course. Anton could almost see the smile on Lord Dietrich's face as he stood at the head of his host, eager to watch as the walls fell. Given the choice, he preferred to be leagues away long before that happened. "How quickly can you reach out to the others?"

"An hour?" said Eckhart, "Some may take convincing."

A fresh chill pierced through Anton's cloak and he fought back a shiver. Outside was silent save for the rustling of branches in the trees across the valley floor. The stars looked brighter than he could remember seeing them before. "Go, the both of you." He had been stationed at this castle for over a decade, never staying in one place longer than a year or so before that. Even as a child his parents kept to the road. In a way this was the one place he could call home. "I want them ready before dawn." The scouts needed no further words, leaving Anton alone with the pair of Falhofnan regulars.

An hour. Coin would be an issue, but there were plenty of towns and traders along the eastern road. They would do. He turned to the soldiers still standing by the fire, their spears resting safely against the wall a few feet away. "How much is your loyalty worth?"

10

He underestimated how much strength the spell would require to maintain. More than once the elves behind him had asked if he wanted to hand over the reins. As much as Kris' wearied limbs wanted him to say yes, how could he pass up this view?

Eight stags carved similarly to the figurine Thysilar had given him as a child were tied together in two rows, a single leather strap stretching down each towards the front of the sleigh. Kris' own stag took the front left position, its broken antler marking it out from the rest. He kept his hold tight on the reins, hoping the weather would hold up. Navigation was difficult enough without having to worry about flying through a storm. *Flying. I'm actually flying.* Estelle would never believe it. Hell, he was still having trouble believing it. In all the stories he was told and the dozens more he had read himself, none of the heroes accomplished anything like this. *Probably because it was foolish to even try.* Kris knew working that level of magick would not be easy, especially considering how much more he still had to learn. How he managed to see it through without killing himself he still did not know. The magick had aided him before, nudged him along the right path, but never to this extent.

The wind shifted and the sleigh rocked hard to the side, threatening to spill the crates stacked behind him over the edge. Nimdor and Fainith worked frantically to keep them in place. Each that fell too hard caused Kris to flinch. *Here's hoping they won't hold a grudge.* Another gust blew past but they were more prepared this time. Kris pulled the stags down and away from the wind stream, balancing them out once the danger had passed. *I could get the hang of this.*

Kris peered down to the landscape below in an attempt to get an idea as to how far along they were. He could make out Crow's Landing a mile or so back, with the Trail of the Vanquished directly ahead. They were getting close. *Good.* Maia and Aelen had taken the remainder of their elves and made for the castle. He gave them three days before completing the spell and joining the march with his own small force. After half a day in the air he spotted the castle.

At the base of the mountain it looked to Kris like a child hugging his mother's leg, afraid to wander too far. The city was dark save for the keep. A handful of lights could be seen the closer they came. "Look," Fainith said, coming up to stand beside Kris. "They're candles. Your friend was true to her word."

She was right. The lights were harder to see from afar but now that they neared the wall he could see small fires flickering in the windows. "Alright. Let's get them ready."

The crates were strapped down to keep the worst of the shifting at bay. Nimdor and his sister unstrapped each bundle, taking care not to disturb their cargo. He moved one to his feet and unclasped a small door at the side of the sleigh. Fainith stood by the rest of the crates in that square, ready to pass them over as needed. "Keep those pets of yours steady." Nimdor picked up the box and held it out over the edge. "Are you ready?"

We'll find out. "Drop them." Kris said. The crate fell from view. He reached out in the same way he had to focus his hearing, only this time his goal was more physical. The intricacies of the power he possessed may have held their secrets but the physical tasks... those he could handle.

At first nothing happened. He could feel the elves' eyes burning holes into him and he ignored them. The crate was falling but he still *felt* it, still knew where it was. Hands made of air and snow gripped wood and metal. A wave of relief flooded over him, nearly severing the link before he composed himself. The chimney stood a few feet over. Kris readjusted, slowing the crate as it touched walls of brick and mortar. Only once it landed safely in the emptied fireplace did he allow himself to relax.

No shouts were heard. No alarms had been sounded. *One down.* "Let's get the next ready. Maia's attack will start soon and I'd prefer not to be the reason she's kept waiting."

The elves smiled in agreement and went to work.

There were sixty miniaturized crates cramped atop the sleigh's narrow surface, each about the size of log cut for the fire and equally tall. By the time the last was delivered Kris felt as though his next step would be his last. His armor was heavy. The snow started to sting his already tired eyes. He wanted to do nothing but fall back and let sleep claim him. *No.* There was still work to be done. A promise to keep.

The stags turned as ordered. Their job was only half-finished. Nimdor reached down to pick up his helm, brushing flakes of snow off of the leather before pulling it down over his head. Beneath their red cloaks their blades waited, but it was not their time yet. Distance remained an ally. *But not forever.* Kris would give them openings to take out as many soldiers as they could. The men closest to the door were a priority. They had their targets. Kris had his. He pulled up on the reins, bringing the stags to a stop. *Come on, come on, come on.*

"There." Fainith said, pointing beyond the wall with her bow.

How she could see the things she did Kris did not know. Even with the help of whatever magick he had the strength for it took a moment for him to spot the single flame. The arrow reached the top of its peak and vanished behind the trees. *Thysilar was wise to suggest her for this.*

She nocked a white-fletched arrow, grinning at her brother. "A friendly contest, then?"

"First to the finish, sweet sister." Nimdor said. The sleigh rested high enough above the keep to ensure they remained hidden. Only elven eyes could see clear to the bottom.

The first two guards were dead before their spears hit the stone. The next two could only turn at the sound as a pair of shafts ended them. Two more fell. Then another two. Each arrow was a kill. The elves stood still as paintings, dealing swift death with every pull.

Kris let the reins fall from his hands, his eyes closed. The spell was not difficult to return to. His mind was focused on little else. Veins of magick twisted this way and that, tangled amongst themselves to reach the desired effect. Creating the knot was the hard part. Something Feltahn would never have let him try. Untying it, he found, was much simpler. The strands slipped free and vanished. As each was undone Kris felt his strength return, piece by piece. He was not close to being at his best, but it was better than he had started to hope. *That's it.* Their fates were in their own hands now.

Below them the soldiers had reached the bell and started ringing it. The barracks' doors were flung open as men half-dressed poured out, pulling on chainmail and boots and juggling weapons as they tried to man the walls. If the attack had been coming from the ground, they may have been able to mount a suitable defense. From Kris' position he could see the holes in their line. It would almost be easy. "Keep me covered." Kris said, and he leapt over the side.

Again he turned to his magick, incorporeal hands catching him at the waist and slowing his descent just enough. He landed on a Falhofnan still struggling with his shirt. The man let out a quick shout as his back was broken. Kris pulled his axe free from the loop at his back, picking up the guard's fallen spear as he rushed the next soldier in line. Three men charged to meet him. Arrows evened the odds. The Falhofnan was too far ahead to notice he was alone and swung his blade wildly, expecting the others to seize upon the opening he would create. Kris parried the blow with his axe and drove the tip of the spear through the man's chest. He pulled it free and reversed his grip, scanning for the closest officer. The spear flew across the wall, avoiding all but its target. He stepped over the soldier's body, ignoring the scream as it faded over the edge.

He could have gotten lost in the melee, swept up as adrenaline flowed and blood was spilled. A dozen men lay dead or dying behind him with dozens more seemingly eager to join them. Who was he to deny them? With sword and axe in hand he cut through spears and parted chainmail. To him every Falhofnan was responsible for Feltahn's death. Each was the face of the burned villages and butchered families. *And each will pay the blood price.* A soldier rushed him as his blade was caught in the body of a recent kill. Kris let it fall and readied his axe as an arrow whizzed past, nicking his ear before burying itself in the Falhofnan's chest. The cut was nothing but brought him out of his own selfishness, back to the larger picture. Fainith. He would have to remember to thank her when this was finished.

The next two arrows acted as markers as the elves began to guide him towards the keep. *Towards the baron.*

11

Ash rained down, mixing with the snow. The ground and houses before him were gray. A dull glow illuminated the night sky, flickering with the wind. *When did the fires start?* Thysilar drew his sword. His leg wobbled beneath his weight. He took a few steadying breaths before opening his eyes. *Alright.* When he heard Kris describe his plan to the gathered elves he felt tempted to strike him, as if his words were those of a man gone mad with fever. The concept of being shrunken down to the size of a wolf pup and dropped down into a smoke stack was not one widely spoken of amongst saner circles. How he managed to convince Maia and the others to go along with it Thysilar could not figure. *But he did it.* The ride was not the most comfortable and the actual process itself left him nauseous, but he did it. Thysilar had his doubts as did most of his other scouts, but he also had his faith. Not in the old gods or whoever it was that looked down at their chaos, but in Kris.

Triandal stepped out from the home they had landed in and took her bow in hand. "Looks like your friend actually did know what he was doing."

"Looks like." Thysilar said. *Now it's our turn.*

The sounds of battle led them along the snow swept roads. More elves emerged around them until just under fifty in all entered the courtyard. A large group of Falhofnan soldiers had formed a barricade, blocking a dozen or so elves from the roads that would take them to the main gates. That was their path. Thysilar silently motioned for them to take to the rooftops. They spread out in a thin circle, surrounding both forces before receiving the order to fire. All sense of discipline vanished and the Falhofnan line crumbled. Arrows came in droves, finding the openings between armor and sinking into the soft flesh beneath. Screams filled the air. Ground forces took advantage then, seizing the opening made by the archers and finishing their grisly work. The elves mended who they could and left those they could not. The gates needed to be opened.

Pockets of resistance were met and dealt with as more elves joined their ranks. Surprise remained on their side, the multiple strikes from all across the city leaving the Falhofnans cut off and disoriented. How could they know where to strike when the enemy was all around them?

Thysilar ran his blade through a Falhofnan's back as his elves on the ground finished those still standing. *We're moving too slowly.* Maia could not be left so close to the wall for long. Muriel stood on the roof of the building beside him, Halfar beside her, readying another arrow. "We're taking too long, wasting too much time on the smaller groups."

"What do you suggest?" Muriel asked, having to shout so she was heard.

That was the question. Triandal took a handful of scouts to check the roads and reported nearly a hundred troops currently moving towards the gate. Combined with the men already stationed there, both on the ground and the wall above, they would be hard fought to secure it. *If those men were drawn away, however....* "We split up."

"Is that wise?" Halfar asked.

"It's all we have," Thysilar said. "Muriel will take a group and make for the gate, as planned. Halfar and I will lead a smaller force and see if we can't get the attention of those reinforcements."

Muriel stared straight ahead without speaking, her mouth opening and closing as though struggling to form words from her thoughts. It was Halfar who at last spoke. "I'll be right behind you."

She smiled in spite of everything. Thysilar thought he saw a single tear slide down her cheek, hiding amidst the snow. "You better." Muriel disappeared into the column of red cloaks, lost to all but Halfar. His eyes followed her wake until the last wisp of crimson rounded the street corner.

"She'll be fine. By now more of us should be well on their way to the gate to join her." Thysilar said. He needed his elves here, focused. No distractions.

Halfar walked past, towards the Falhofnans unknowingly waiting for them. "She always was."

The fire started somewhere along the city's western edge but it had spread far past that now. Flames crept from building to building like the elves ahead of them, lighting the sky. Thysilar would have preferred the dark. *An extra legion or two would also be nice. Yet here we are.* He would have to make due. The Falhofnans were marching through the piling snow in a pair of mismatched columns. They were led by a knight, his plate armor hidden beneath his bearskin cloak. He did what he could to maintain order. It was a decent effort. Those fortunate enough to be in full armor were few, mixed in with those who must have had time to grab only their weapon as the alarm was sounded. It almost wasn't fair.

The knight was the first to fall, an arrow taking him in the side. Then the man next to him.

Panic. Men raised their weapons against invisible foes. Arrows found them regardless. Soldiers on both ends were falling fast, causing the others to shrink back and away, clumping themselves together. "Separate!" one shouted, "They're grouping us in!" But he was just one man and unable to stand against the press of so many bodies.

It was impossible to miss. Falhofnans fell by the dozen. The younger soldiers not hemmed in turned and fled. They were not alone. "Let them run." Thysilar said, "Don't waste your arrows." Some were able to return fire but none found their mark. *We're winning,* Thysilar dared to think. He never saw the shadows.

Triandal cried out, clutching her shin where a black-fletched arrow had pierced both armor and flesh. She lost her balance on the sloped shingles and slid. Her hands lashed out for anything she could grasp, but found nothing. Thysilar could only watch as she fell. He heard the sound of her body striking the cobblestone through the din below.

Snow crunched underfoot as he leapt down to lead the ground assault. His sword bit flesh, sending out blood in a wide arc, stark against the white of the snow. The man fell with a whisper, swallowed by the chorus of swords and axes. Thysilar chose his next target. His blade rang out against the man's shield and pushed him back a step, his arms shaking. He was reckless, eager. He would not make the same mistake twice. The soldier kept his shield up and charged the elf, forcing Thysilar to move or be rundown. It was a solid move, but Thysilar could recognize a fresh recruit when he saw one. Instead of back straight as he was expected to do, he spun his body around the length of the shield, positioning himself to deliver the death blow. The boy panicked, flailing his spear around and clipping Thysilar behind the ear. Stars dotted his vision and his footing failed him. The cut still healing on his leg flared and threatened to bring him down further. He looked up to the face of his would-be killer and could not choke down the chuckle. *Laid low by a child. At least death will spare me the embarrassment back at camp.* He kept his eyes open, refusing not to experience his final moments.

The look of surprise on the boy's face was pure. He could not understand why his strength left him, even as he fell to the snow, his lifeblood spreading beneath him. Thysilar looked all around the rooftops until he saw him. Halfar already had another arrow ready but hesitated a moment to offer a brief nod. A moment was all that was needed. The Falcon pulled Halfar's head back with enough force to break bone, pushing his blade through the elf's back to emerge out from his chest. Halfar's arrow flew wide, his bow falling to the battle below. He did not struggle, as so many would. He knew his death when it was shown to him. That did not mean he was useless. With the strength he still had he locked his leg around the Falcon's and took hold of his wrist. The last look he gave was a smile as he pushed himself off the ledge, dragging his killer with him to the cold, unforgiving ground.

There was no time for mourning. Not now. *Get up. Get up and do your duty.* Halfar did not make that sacrifice for Thysilar to die on his knees. With anger in his heart and a shout on his lips he rose. Wherever he walked, men died. Some held their own, even managing to draw blood. They fell all the same. It was not until his leg gave out completely that he allowed himself to stop. The world was blurring, losing its color. He had lost too much blood.

His elves were dying. The remaining Falhofnans had regrouped, their archers laying down cover as the rest started back for the gate. The Falcons could deal with the rest. There was nothing more he could do. He hoped they bought Muriel enough time. *The Falcons, however...* His hands searched the ground around him and grasped a bow. Half a dozen arrows still sat in his quiver. *Strength enough.*

A northern wind blew past, carrying the scent of pine and wood smoke. Back home they would be gathered around a fire, bellies warm, drinking wine and swapping stories. Estelle would have some sort of pie no matter how full they claimed to be. *And Kris would be the one telling them, we, the ones with a child's curiosity.* Thysilar breathed that air in deep, wishing he could hold it in and never let it go.

12

The keep was deserted. Kris walked through the unlit halls, sword out before him. As sudden as the attack had been it was unlikely the baron would allow himself to be left unprotected. *If it was me, I'd have an ambush in place.* He passed the kitchens and servants quarters. The dining hall was left almost entirely bare. A single mug remained, tipped on its side at the edge of the table. Even the heraldry was gone. The material alone would fetch a high price to the right buyer. *Why would he allow any of this? Has he accepted defeat so entirely?* He reached the base of the spiral stairway and looked back over his shoulder. Since he was told the first stories regarding this castle he had always wondered what it would be like to walk its halls, take in the artwork decorating the walls. *Never did I imagine it like this.* A cold had settled here, one he could not shake off.

He took the stairs two at a time, his anxiety rising with each. There were no torches or rails but he needed either. He slowed as he neared the top, unwilling to be taken by surprise. This floor was smaller than the others with only two doors that Kris could see. The first was the baron's personal chambers. He scanned the area left to right and was ready to leave when he heard a sound from under the bed. Returning the axe to his belt, he crouched down to the floor and lifted the ruffles to find a young woman staring at him. Her eyes were red. She sobbed softly, wiping at the wetness around her nose as she tried to push herself back further.

"It's alright. I'm not going to hurt you." Kris said.

The woman hesitated, glancing back to the other end of the bed as though for help.

"Look," he brushed aside the hair around his ears to reveal their rounded edges. "I'm not an elf. I can help." He still wore the crimson cloak but hoped in the dark, with her less than attentive state, it would go unnoticed. Her sobbing eased but still she refused to move. *Fine.* "You can stay there. You'll be safe, out of sight. Just tell me where he is."

"I-I'm not sure my lord would –." she started to say.

"I was sent here to protect our lord. The city is under attack and there are those who will use this confusion to get to him. Do you want that to happen?"

She looked confused, as though unsure how she should answer. Her head slowly shook.

"Good. Neither do I. Please, where is the baron?" Kris asked again, feeling his patience wane.

The young woman let go of the sheet long enough to point, her hand trembling.

His study. "Thank you, my lady." He gave her the most reassuring smile he could before the ruffle fell. At least now he knew.

The door to the study was closed, with a dull glow peeking out from the space at the floor. He put his ear to the wood but heard nothing. *Alright.* Kris stepped away from the door a few steps, planted his feet, and kicked the door in. The fireplace was burning brightly, but powerless against the cold that rushed out to greet him.

"Finally. I was beginning to wonder if you had gotten lost." The elf turned from the window, his hands crossed behind his back. "It was quite rude of them not to leave a single torch before scurrying for their holes like so many rats."

Kris tightened the grip on his sword as his anger rose. He had left him whole during their first encounter and Feltahn was killed. The elf would not be so lucky again. "Where is the baron?"

"You're looking at him," he said, making a grand gesture with his arms before bowing. "Baron Jak, the First of his Name. And the Last."

A host of questions flooded his mind and he had a hard time deciding which to start with. Among them all was the gnome's face, as he chose to remember him. Not the cold form they buried in the mountain. He made a promise to Estelle. *And to Feltahn.* If this Jak was calling himself Baron it could only mean Gerold was dead. It was hard to ignore the disappointment. This whole venture was centralized around bringing down the Baron. With Gerold dead, that job was finished. *Just leaves one more.* "I hoped you'd still be here."

Jak smiled at that. "Of course. The gnome. It was valiant the way he protected you. Still, he served his purpose. My message brought you here, after all." He took slow steps forward. Figures moved within the shadows on either side. "Now, what is it you wanted to speak to me about?"

Kris thrust his hand forward as a cloud of ice coalesced around it. He poured his will into it, fuelled by the anger still very much present in his mind, propelling the cloud towards Jak. The elf stood perfectly still as the spell dissipated, harmlessly passing over his chest.

"Ice," he said, looking down at where the attack had struck. "Ice I am intimately aware of." Jak's spell mirrored Kris', only when it hit, it did so with far greater force.

Kris crashed into the desk behind him, continuing over the top to the floor. He dropped his sword almost instantly and could see it then, lying by the fire. *Might as well be a mile away.* He heard Jak's footsteps getting closer. They were not alone. He needed a plan. The questions previously clouding his mind were gone as adrenaline kicked in. A handful of options came to the fore, but none of them brought much confidence. Magick was pushed to the side. Whatever talents he had, Jak could outmatch. How, Kris was unsure, but there would be plenty of time for such questions once the night was done. Instead of willing the magick out he focused on keeping it in, letting it amplify his entire body. He opened his eyes feeling greater than he had in years. *And stronger.* He stood, drawing Berengar's axe as he turned to find Jak flanked by a pair of the largest hounds he had ever seen.

They were not natural. That much was apparent. Carved from pure ice, they moved through both the light and the dark as though belonging to neither. Black eyes stared at him. Sharp teeth glistened with their hunger. They wanted to kill him. But they wouldn't. Not without their master's word.

Good. At least they're obedient monsters. His plan had not taken them into account but there was little he could alter that would make much difference. Kris kicked out at the desk with his newfound strength, sending it gliding across the stone toward the elf and his pets. Without waiting to see the result he rushed after it, bringing his axe in line with the elf's neck. Jak leapt, clearing both desk and Kris, twisting his body about to land facing the pair.

The hound to his left barreled into Kris as he stopped just shy of hitting the desk. Its claw raked across his shoulder and chest, getting through his armor and cloak enough to draw blood. He pushed the haft of his axe against the hound's throat and lifted it off and away. The second wasted no time to seize the opening. Moving faster than even he anticipated he swung the axe wide and low, catching the beast along the head and taking its ear. Chips of ice hit the floor. It showed no signs of pain and kept moving. Kris fell beneath its weight, bringing the axe up to stop the rows of teeth from clamping around his throat. He could not keep up the defense forever, he knew. It snapped again and again but its jaws never found their mark. *For now.* Avoiding another bite a thought came to him. It was so obvious he felt like letting the beast take a bite out of him. *Just a small one.*

Kris put the flat of his boot against its underbelly and let one hand go. The hound got closer, seizing the chance. The fire was further than he thought. His fingertips brushed wood and he scrambled for a better grip. Powerful jaws opened to end him. He took the burning log in his hand, ignoring the pain, and jammed it down the hound's throat. Steam rose from its mouth as it whined, frantically shaking its head as it backed away in fear. However powerful the spell that gave them life, it could not overcome nature.

The hound started to break down, its body melting from within. The remaining beast watched as black eyes pooled and seeped into the wood. It moved with caution, steadily circling him.

Smart. Kris risked a glance at Jak. A playful smirk crossed his face and Kris saw why. He conjured another spell, identical to the first.

Glass shattered as Kris was thrown through the window. Snow was all around. The fall should have killed him. He thanked the magick for that. As it was he cracked a few ribs, the ankle of the foot he landed on, and the wrist he put down to try and spread some of the impact. *Fool. Even a dog made of ice knew to learn from the damn fight.* He rolled onto his knees, using his left arm to keep him from collapsing. The spell he cast had run dry. He could barely keep his eyes open.

"Look at you. Broken. Beaten. You have enough power to level an entire city and here you sit, so easily bested." Kris did not see how the elf or his pet made it down so fast but it did not surprise him. "Why did it choose you?"

Kris tried to stand but was pushed back down. His words died in his throat. "I don't know." he whispered.

"What? Speak clearly, boy. Your elves are making a racket." His hound snarled and inched closer.

"I don't know." Kris said again. And it was the truth. "I'm no one special. Just a babe found in the forest who would have died if not for the kindness of an elf." Again he tried to stand and again Jak kept him down.

"It was meant for me. Not for him. Nor for you. But me. I doubt that old gnome bothered to tell you that." Jak turned as a building collapsed nearby, the sound like thunder echoing through the night. "All of this, the blood, the death, all of it is placed at his feet. The cycle of greed and obsession has gone unchecked for too long. But no longer." He took Kris by the neck and lifted him as though he was a child. "I'll start with the elves, I think. My people deserve their vengeance. I'll be kind. Kinder than they deserve, I promise you. This, I fear, is going to hurt."

Icy fingers clawed their way through his stomach and Kris screamed. He struck with all he had, each blow feeling as though the elf was made of stone.

"The more you struggle the harder it will be."

Kris bit his tongue, filling his mouth with the taste of copper. There was no more he could do. Not like this. The pain made it almost impossible to think of anything else. *Jak will rip the magick out of me and use it... Of course.* Jak's spell was nearing his heart. He would only have one chance.

The spell was laid out perfectly in his mind. All it needed was his will to grant it life. *However much of it I have left.* He could only hope it would be enough. Kris gripped the elf's forearm with his injured arm to steady himself. Compared to the pain already wracking his body his wrist was easy to ignore. Blue light reflected off Jak's face and for a moment the playful smile was gone. Kris felt his consciousness falter as he poured the last of his will to his palm. With a howl loud enough to pierce the battle still raging within the city walls, he raised his good arm and shoved the sphere of green light into Jak's mouth.

The elf pulled back instantly and Kris fell to the ground. "What did you do to me?"

Kris only smiled.

Jak tugged at the collar of his shirt until it ripped and then moved on to his skin. Already his nails had drawn blood. "Kill him!" he shouted. The hound studied its prey, still cautious, but did not wait long before advancing.

He would have accepted death then. His promise was kept. The elves would be inside the walls in force now. Even without the element of surprise still on their side Maia would be able to bring the Falhofnans still fighting to heel. The war, for all intents and purposes, was over. *I've done my part.*

The hound reached his feet and snarled at the meal to come as an arrow pierced its eye. The snarl turned to a whimper. It tried frantically to pull the arrow free with its teeth when another whistled through the air and blinded it. Kris turned to see Nimdor descending the stairs, bloodied blade in hand, with Fainith quickly following. The inner wall was won. It took three swings to bring the beast down.

Fainith dropped her bow and looped her arm under Kris' shoulder. "Can you stand?"

"Yes, just don't go anywhere." he answered. Nimdol checked that he was alright and moved to deal with Jak. "Don't." Kris said, stopping the elf where he stood. "It's finished." He shrugged off the elf's help.

Jak had fallen to his knees, his skin drying out and turning pale. His hands hung limp by his sides. "What did…." His voice was faint, the words trailing off. Kris could see his legs had started to sink into the ground.

"I gave you what you wanted." Kris said, his voice still sore. "This, what you're feeling right now, is magick in its most pure form. Natural. I almost laughed. The whole time it was staring right at me." He crouched down to meet the elf's eyes. This was why magick existed. Not to destroy, as Jak and the elves before him would have used it, but to create. To give life. "My mother used to tell me stories about men who ran off with vengeance in their hearts. The paths they took would vary but the destination was always the same."

"Two graves." Jak said, his hands merging into the dirt. The spell was nearly complete.

"Two graves." Kris repeated.

"You'll need more." The elf's laugh was dry as his skin grew hard and cracked. Beneath him roots dug deep, branches sprouting up as the base of a great tree took shape. Jak could do nothing as the wood enveloped him. He kept his eyes solely on Kris, even as the rest of his body was lost to the tree. They were the last to be taken.

Kris stared at the tree, losing track of time. "Have we taken the gate?"

"We didn't have to." It was Muriel who answered. She was wounded. All of them were. Her right arm she kept close to her side. Ash stained her face, washed away in places where tears had fallen. "Apparently there was a turncoat amongst them. Once he saw our forces marshaled he ordered the gates opened."

"What?" The thought made no sense to him. After everything, all the killing and the bloodshed, one man simply opened the gates. *Why couldn't he have come to us earlier?*

"Maia has him at the wall. He wasn't alone. Over a hundred of his Falcons surrendered with him."

"Has he said anything?" Kris asked.

"Just that he'd like to speak with you." Muriel said, "Something about a reward."

13

"Gold and silver!" the man shouted again. He had hair redder than any Estelle had seen, with a beard that went down to his rounded torso. A group had gathered around the large box he stood on. *One of Kris'*, she noted. "The mountain is filled with deposits untouched for centuries. Any man who accompanies me will return with riches enough to retire a king!" A few volunteered. *And less will make it back.* The forests had only just opened for safe travel with the peace Kris' victory brought and already they searched for other ways to die. She kept her hood up and continued toward the keep.

Efforts had been made to rebuild the homes and buildings damaged during the battle. Estelle walked past four identical piles of charred wood and knew at least twice as many more were scattered throughout the city. *The lower quarter especially.* That half had not seen much battle but the fires spread fast, latching on to the straw most of the homes there had been roofed with. She meant to see the damage herself before she left.

Elves stood by the main doors and atop the surrounding walls. Their presence was something the people of the city would have to get used to. She looked past the tall oak to a smaller tree, still young. None questioned as she walked past. Servants both human and elf roamed the halls, preparing food or otherwise performing some task or another. She gave each a warm smile as she passed them by, stopping at the hall as a group were working to hang a new banner at the back wall. *Not new at all,* Estelle saw as she looked closer. The colors were faded, the strings of the embroidered stag loose and unkempt. Holes likely chewed by moths dotted the surface. But still, there was a beauty to it. *I'm surprised he didn't have it burned.* It had been over a century at least since she saw it last.

The stairs left her legs tired and a terrible ache settled in her knee. It always acted up in the cold. *And this winter has been cold indeed.* "Oh, I'm sorry."

A young woman with fiery red hair clutched the bed sheet to her chest as her face reddened. More than a few empty wine bottles lay scattered across the floor. The smile was full of embarrassment. "No, no, it's alright. I wasn't sure when you'd be coming. He's in the study."

Estelle tried her most polite smile and continued down the hall. Hundreds of books lined the walls, resting on shelves where there was space, and in piles wherever they could fit. A small stack stood on top of the desk. Two texts were open beside it with a leather bound book filled with mostly blank pages beside them. Kris stood by the fire in a robe the color of sage. His beard had grown thicker. *He could use a shave.* "She seems nice."

"I was hoping to have a dinner where you could've met more...."

"Clothed?"

Kris turned, smiling. "I'm sorry, mother."

"There's no need to apologize. I was young once." Estelle said, glad to see her son happy. "She's very beautiful."

"Thank you." Kris said. "How was the trip?"

"Long. I look forward to being back by a fire and my own bed."

"I hope the room I have for you is comfortable enough."

"It will be." Estelle said. "I saw the tree outside."

Kris was silent. She could almost see the scowl through his mop of hair.

"He would have liked it."

"Mother," Kris said, turning away from the fire. His eyes looked weary. "I –"

"Don't. There's no need. She stood on the tips of her toes to kiss his cheek. "No one could have made him do anything he did not want."

"It was my command that –."

"I said don't." Estelle moved the open books aside revealing a half-finished drawing of what appeared to be another castle. "What's this?"

Kris walked up behind her and turned the parchment over. She could smell alcohol on his breath. "A new project. It's just the rough sketch. There's still much to be done here first."

"So you'll be staying then."

He nodded. "The council offered me a position. It's where I belong. Might be there's something in one of these books that can tell me about my parents."

Might be. "The people are lucky to have you."

"How long will you be staying?"

"A few days. It's been… a long time since I've been to the city. I'd like to see how much has changed." She realized that was a dumb thing to say considering the city had just been through a siege.

"I didn't know you'd been here before." Kris said. He let the words linger between them before moving on. "We'll have to arrange that dinner before you leave then. It'll be nice. Quiet. Like before."

"I'd like that."

Estelle showed herself out, not prepared for the cold she should have expected. A silence had crept over the city, as though everyone had chosen this one moment to stop and marvel at the sunset. Alone, for the first time in months, she felt at peace.

She looked up, unable to mask her smile. The pale oak was wreathed by an orange glow, its limbs bristling in the dying wind.

ABOUT THE AUTHOR

A reader since his elementary school days, lover of stories and all things Christmas, Derek Feuti turned to telling stories of his own and never looked back. It was only a matter of time before the two came together. He lives in Rhode Island, absorbing everything from comic books to autobiographies. Kringle is his first novel.

You can follow him on Facebook and Twitter (@DJcreso) where you can find out what projects he's working on now, as well as the origins of that nickname.

www.derekfeuti.com

www.ingramcontent.com/pod-product-compliance
Lightning Source LLC
Chambersburg PA
CBHW072227170626
46813CB00003B/1118